THE LIGHTHOUSE MURDER

Elaine J. Anderson

authorHOUSE®

AuthorHouse™
1663 Liberty Drive
Bloomington, IN 47403
www.authorhouse.com
Phone: 1-800-839-8640

Published by AuthorHouse   10/09/2014

ISBN: 978-1-4969-4414-6 (sc)
ISBN: 978-1-4969-4415-3 (hc)
ISBN: 978-1-4969-4643-0 (e)

Library of Congress Control Number: 2014918175

Chapter 1

JAKE SOBBED AS HE HELD Arthur in his arms. "Wake up! Wake up!" he pleaded to the still body. Tears streamed down his face. Dawn was soon to come, bringing light to the beach they rested on.

The two men had been flying high on drugs and alcohol. They had been unaware of the time of day as the sun set in the west, enflaming the sky and reflecting strongly on the lighthouse behind them. Erotic sex games had become a highlight to their weekends together in Provincetown at the tip of Cape Cod. Only this time it was different.

Finally, Jake realized what had happened. He had tried and tried to loosen the belt around Arthur's neck in time when Arthur signaled, "Enough!" but he wasn't in time. Still cradling Arthur, Jake lowered him to the sandy beach, took his belt lying next to Arthur and replaced it around his own waist, and then gently covered the lifeless body with sand to keep him warm.

Jake was coming down from his drug high and a night on the beach. "I need to get out of here," he murmured to himself in the eerie silence that engulfed him as the waves pounded the beach. He knew now that he was in deep trouble.

He got up from his hollow in the dune and brushed the sand from his knees. He trudged through the sand in the direction of the moors and the breakwater back to the west end of Provincetown. A ribbon of morning light was appearing on the eastern horizon as Jake neared the empty streets of the town. He saw a distant jogger, and no one else, as he made his way to Arthur's apartment on Court Street. He was planning to clear out any trace of his visit. While he was cleaning up the apartment— dishes, glasses, clothes, and sex toys—he had a thought. It would be difficult to trace him to Arthur, but if they did get close for some reason, Jake remembered that his brother Jimmy had left a pair of swim shorts and a gold chain engraved with the date he graduated from high school and the initials DDS in the glove compartment of Jake's SUV. Jake moved quickly to retrieve the items from his car. He brought them back to the apartment and placed them in a drawer in Arthur's bedroom.

Framing Jimmy was the perfect answer. Jake grew up in the projects of New York City with his twin brother and single mother. Jake was born first by several minutes, making him the older brother, a fact he reminded Jimmy of frequently. The boys were a handful of energy and mischief at home and at school. Jake helped his young widowed mother carry groceries up the tenement stairs. Jake made sure that Jimmy got the heaviest bag to carry. Jake was convinced that Jimmy was his mother's favorite. No matter how often Jake was told by his mother that she loved them equally, he knew better. He remembered the birthday when his mother had baked two special cakes for them. His cake had a small burned edge to it; Jimmy's cake was perfect. He remembered the time when his gift was a plain jacket and Jimmy's had a blue logo on it. He remembered how his mother held Jimmy to make him feel better after a fall as she scolded Jake for pushing Jimmy.

Jake had spent his life tormenting Jimmy and framing him for his own misdeeds. Jake's anger and jealousy about what he took for truth had manifested itself into a raging temper. His mother often had to remind Jake to "be nice to your brother." Yes, framing Jimmy was the ultimate revenge.

Jimmy was mild-mannered, gentle, and giving. As an adult Jimmy focused on his dental practice in the city, played his guitar, and enjoyed his favorite jazz club. His strong character allowed him to develop into a successful man and dental surgeon. Jimmy's successes just made Jake more envious.

As young boys they played together in the projects where they grew up. When the boys grew older, got driver's licenses, and eventually a car, they would occasionally drive to the Jersey Shore to see the ocean and play on the sandy beaches. Jake loved the smell of the salt air and seaweed, while Jimmy was fascinated with birds, fish, and whales. Jake had become very rich. No one was sure how that happened. He said that he was in sales. What he sold was never very clear. He bought his mother a brand-new house in a gated community in upstate New York, far from the projects. With his unexplained wealth, he bought himself a luxury SUV and a condo overlooking the Hudson River, and rented the penthouse apartment in New York City with his wife of three years, Cathy, a girl from a wealthy, prominent New York advertising family.

The twins drifted apart as they grew older, but through the years they had traveled to Cape May, Atlantic City, Newport, and Provincetown at the tip of Cape Cod, Massachusetts. Jimmy's favorite place to go whale watching was Provincetown. He'd hitch a ride with Jake whenever he knew that his brother was headed to the cape. Although he did not own a car, sometimes he'd go on his own by bus.

In Provincetown, the boys would always split up. Jimmy would go on his coveted whale watch. Jake preferred renting a bike and heading to the nude male beach that lay hidden in the national seashore dunes.

As Jake closed the trunk of his packed car, he remembered a weekend a year ago when he met Arthur Milne at a tea dance. He was first drawn to a silhouette against the bright watery backdrop off the deck. He had moved closer to see the dark hair, brown eyes, and tanned torso. He saw that Arthur was full of energy and promise.

"Your next drink is from me," he whispered as he leaned into the end of the bar nearest the deck rail where Arthur stood to call to the bartender. Arthur smiled.

After drinks and intimate dancing on the deck, they had left the tea dance for the west end of town and a romantic moonlit walk across the breakwater to Long Point Beach.

Holding hands, the two talked, as new lovers do.

"I always wanted to walk out here," Arthur told him. "It's a dream come true."

"I never knew that you could walk out here. I knew about the water shuttle from the pier," Jake had told him.

"We're really lucky tonight with the clear sky and bright moon," Arthur shared.

"It feels like a fantasy. I'm floating," Jake had said, bringing Arthur close as they embraced in a long, tender kiss. Later, in the nude, they had fooled around under the moonlight in the water, shared a towel that Arthur had, and spent the night together cuddled in the sand.

"You must know that I have never been this happy," Jake had confessed to Arthur on that first night. Long Point Beach near the lighthouse had become a special place for them.

3

Until meeting Arthur Milne, Jake had carefully developed his acting skills for everyday living. He played a role, one he wrote for himself—married, successful, happy. He performed with confidence, bravado, and charm. "This is my beautiful wife," or "Not many men have my good fortune ... I mean, terrific partner," he'd brag mindlessly. Meeting Arthur made everything different. Jake had finally acknowledged his bisexuality, his secret. It was addictive. He wanted more excitement from this relationship. Drugs, sex, and alcohol became so alluring that he found himself spending more and more time away at "business meetings" to be with this tender, romantic man, Arthur.

"You can't miss carnival," Arthur had said. "Can you come for circuit weekend?" he asked. "You must come for family week; this is so special. You'll see gay families, straight families, and children of all ages. Maybe you can just move here!" Arthur had mentioned.

Jake's wife believed his convincing stories of lucrative business meetings and more wealth for the family they planned to have one day. "Honey, I just got a call from a client. I need to go to close a deal. You know how I hate to leave you alone. It is too lucrative a deal to put off, though," he'd tell his wife, Cathy. It sounded like a mantra. "You know how much I love you," or "There is no one in this world I'd rather spend my life with," he'd lie to her over and over again. He had made false flight and hotel reservations in Connecticut, Pennsylvania, and Canada, only to cancel them later. "I just don't understand the frequency of these weeklong, midweek, and weekend absences," Cathy would complain. He'd bring her perfume and flowers, take her to expensive restaurants, and act as though everything was okay.

Jake knew today that things were far from okay. He set up an alibi that would place him far away from Provincetown on this fateful weekend. His wife believed that he was in Philadelphia. He had a friend there where he had stayed on other "business" trips. Jake phoned to set up a visit on his way home, so that he would have indeed been in Philadelphia.

Today as he stood at the door of Arthur's condo in Provincetown, he started to cry. He needed to get hold of himself and get out of the place quickly and unseen. He slipped out of Arthur Milne's condo, got into his car—a silver Cadillac SUV with New York plates—and quietly left the cape for Philadelphia as a sob rose in his throat.

Chapter 2

I N PROVINCETOWN, SMALL BOATS BOBBED on their moorings in the harbor. A few puff-clouds gathered on the horizon of an otherwise solid blue sky. The sun was bright in the east as it rose for another day. Across the bay on a spit of sand stood a black-and-white lighthouse framed against the deep green sea. The famous Long Point Light, built in 1827, was all that remained of the original settlement of fishermen, called Long Point Village. The settlers decided to leave Long Point and took most of their houses with them, about thirty houses in all, by floating them across the harbor to Provincetown. Today nothing remains, except for the lighthouse and an earthen mound, the last remnant from an earlier military post.

On this day yellow crime tape rattled in the wind and stretched from the base of the lighthouse in a wide sweep across the sand mound and back again. The police chief, Gerald Jeter, knelt down next to the scantily clothed body that lay with swim trunks and a cotton shirt neatly tucked in around the chest in the sand at the foot of the lighthouse. Pulling the shirt away from the neck and shoulders and feeling for a pulse, the police chief looked up at his detective and to the national seashore ranger.

"He's dead. Notify the state police. Considering the marks around his neck, I think we have a suspicious death." The chief surveyed the area around the victim before rising to his feet. "That will trigger the forensics team and the medical examiner." The detective reached for her phone.

A flurry of activity ensued around the area as more crime tape was put into position, warning onlookers to stay their distance. The chief, detective Sylvia Santos, and national seashore ranger Rex Sanders were all intent on preserving the crime scene until the arrival of the state police forensic investigator and medical examiner. Sylvia Santos took a picture of the form partially buried in the sand. Other than the splashing of the water at the edge of the beach, the only sound was the chief as he whispered, "Such a tragedy."

Within minutes a state police helicopter hovered overhead and landed downwind from the crime scene, churning up sand and surf with its blades. The forensic investigator and the medical examiner climbed out of the copter, now perched on the sand in dune grass above the high-tide mark. They made their way through the vegetation to the crime scene, where they saw the trio gathered.

"Over here," called the chief.

The medical examiner headed to him, and they shook hands. "Good to see you, Jerry." The ME, Stephanie Isaac, moved past the crime tape toward the body.

"Sad to say, this is probably the only way I ever get to my favorite fishing village," the ME told the chief as she moved to observe the body. She knelt down close to the figure and looked for obvious marks and signs for the time of death.

"We need to get the remains back to the morgue," she announced. "Apart from the strap mark on his neck, I'll be able to give you more precise information after the autopsy."

After the forensic specialist had taken photographs of the deceased and surrounding area, the go-ahead was given to the detectives to place the corpse into the body bag, zip it closed, and move it to the helicopter.

"He had no identification on him," the Provincetown detective, Sylvia Santos, told the examiner. The afternoon wind was picking up, blowing stinging sand at their faces.

"No ID always makes for a challenge. We'll check for missing person reports and fingerprint matches," the ME said, rising from her kneeling position. She looked around the site and shouted to Sally Acker, the state forensic investigator, returning from the police copter toward the crime tape, "See what you can find! I need to get back to the lab. Check in with me tomorrow afternoon." She headed past the remaining police investigators to the helicopter.

The chief followed the medical examiner a short way from the crime tape. "First impressions?" He stubbed his boot into the rough sand.

"My gut tells me that we have a suspicious death, possibly by suffocation. I'll have more for you in a few days," Stephanie answered, shielding her eyes from the sun and sand while moving toward the copter.

The chief turned against the wind and blowing sand to join the remaining team to search for anything that could help the investigation. Trying to find evidence in the sand wasn't easy! To complicate the search, the wind velocity was creating the impression of a sandstorm as it swept the beach. A rough sea was rising from the calm bay earlier that day.

"This is impossible," complained Santos. "We'll never find anything in this wind."

"I agree." Sally Acker, the forensic investigator, pulled her hood over her head and zipped up her jacket.

"Let's get back to the pier and call it a day," Santos called over the wind.

"Suits me." Sally rose from a crouched position at her observation point near the base of the lighthouse. She was carrying an engraved wristwatch in an evidence bag as she moved toward the group.

"See you later," shouted the seashore ranger Rex Sanders from an all-terrain vehicle, moving away from the area along a spit of beach back toward the mainland.

Jeter and Santos gave a wave to acknowledge the ranger and called to the investigator from the State ME's office to come to the patrol boat, dwarfed by the lighthouse and anchored in shallow water.

The harbormaster, Burt Randell, was waiting in the patrol boat. The others moved in the shallow, turbulent water to the stern of the vessel, and with assistance from the harbormaster, one by one, lifted themselves up a short ladder onto the deck of a twenty-four-foot V-hull patrol boat. Each of the three people secured a life jacket around themselves in preparation for the rough ride across the bay. The harbormaster took the helm, started the engine, and gave the chief, now on the bow of the boat, a shout to bring in the anchor. Moments later they were headed away from the beach where the body had been and across the choppy bay to the pier in the center of town.

"We haven't met before." Acker extended her hand to the chief. "I'm Sally Acker, the state forensic specialist in the medical examiner's office."

The Provincetown police chief clung tightly to the boat railing behind the captain's chair as he and Sally tried to converse. She sat seated next to the captain. They shouted above the noise of the motor and the wind, while taking on the sea splash.

"I'll be staying the night in Truro with my aunt and returning to the site in the morning," she informed him during the choppy wet ride.

"I'm pleased to have you working on this homicide with us. It isn't often we have a murder, much less one with no ID," the chief told her. "How long will it take to get the report?" he asked. Time was critical. No one wanted the trail to go cold.

"I'll stay a few days to complete the investigation with your detective," she answered. "The lab is really backed up, but we'll move as fast as we can." She turned around in the seat and watched the town and its pier come closer through the churning waters.

"Sally, will you need a ride over tomorrow, or are you going to hike the long way out to the lighthouse?" called the harbormaster, maneuvering the boat to cut across the waves in the rough bay.

"Yes, I'll need a ride. Do you think it'll be calmer tomorrow morning?" Sally called out against the wind as another wave broke across the bow of the boat.

"Can't guarantee that, but I'll be glad to bring you over."

Sally watched the harbormaster as he guided the patrol boat into dock at the pier. The chief assisted, tying the ropes from the boat to the dock and helping the riders off the rocking boat and onto the stable pier.

When all four people were off the vessel, the harbormaster pulled the hose from its holder on the pier, turned on the water, and began to hose down the salty boat.

They all had taken on sea spray and felt chilled. For a few minutes all four of them milled about until the chief took control and led the group off the pier in search of fried clams and beer at a local clam shack on Commercial Street.

****

The news of the murder at the lighthouse raced through the small fishing village as fire races through tinder.

"Damn drugs," a storekeeper told his Portuguese friend after hearing the rumor on the dock.

"No, sounds more like booze, and he probably drowned because he was so drunk," a tanned, curly black-haired fisherman said.

"Then why'd the cop say murder?" asked the storekeeper.

"Cause he don't know nothing yet."

"Who was it anyway? Did he live here?"

"Don't know. Nobody ain't talkin'. But I got a hunch," said the fisherman, moving away from the store toward Lopes Square.

"Hey, wait. What's yer hunch?" the storekeeper cried to his friend from the shop doorway.

"Can't say yet," he shouted back and kept walking.

For those folks in town who hadn't heard the rumor, the bold headline in the local paper the next morning got everyone's attention: **Local Man Murdered at Long Point Lighthouse**.

****

Meanwhile, Jake Dimmer was wining and dining his wife in an upscale restaurant in Manhattan.

"This is getting to be a habit, Jake. Every time you return from a business trip, we go someplace really special. If I didn't know you better, I'd think you were acting out of guilt," she told him with an endearing smile.

Jake flushed at the statement. He was sure that she didn't know his secret. Just the same, he was very uncomfortable this time. Things had gone very wrong on his weekend sojourn.

He took her hand and with a nervous twitch at the corner of his mouth whispered, "You know that I love you, don't you?"

With a smile she answered, "Yes. I miss you when you go away."

Jake had been drinking more than usual during dinner. He needed a diversion from his thoughts. "Are you feeling up to a nightclub and some dancing tonight?" he asked his wife.

"I'd love to," she answered, noticing the spark of romance that always flared after his business trips. She felt herself fighting off a familiar, nagging feeling of doubt about these frequent absences; *could there be another woman?*

An hour later, even holding his wife close, feeling her warmth against him and moving with the rhythm of her body in time with the music gave him little solace. The vivid memory of forty-eight hours earlier on Cape Cod in the shadow of a lighthouse in Provincetown haunted him, and no amount of dancing could drive it from his mind.

After dancing and drinking more than he should have, they went to a piano bar and sang along with the piano player and guests for hours. Cathy loved spending time with Jake, even though the last year of absences had been trying. He was traveling more. He was drinking more. He was conversing less. Yes, she was worried that it was another woman.

Cathy Astor Dimmer had watched his deterioration accelerate over the past year of their three-year marriage. They had met at a golf club fund-raiser in Tarrytown, New York. He was handsome and she was rich, the debutante daughter of a prominent upstate New York advertising family. She was taken in by his stories of the travels and enterprises he had done. He was well-groomed head to toe, had the gift of gab, and had captured Cathy's heart. Cathy and Jake had an elaborate wedding at the Astor family home in the Hamptons. Jake had hit pay dirt. He had achieved his dream, a very rich wife.

****

Jake had done the unthinkable. He had killed his lover, and he had framed his twin by planting a gold chain and swim shorts at Arthur Milne's apartment. It would only be a matter of time until authorities tracked down Jimmy as a suspect. After all, Jimmy was single, spent a lot of time fawning over their mother, and frequently visited Provincetown. He fit the gay profile. He would have no alibi. It was perfect.

Even so, Jake had convinced himself that he would be the hero in all of this. He'd be able to help Jimmy get good legal advice and therapy for his "problem." He fantasized that if his mother believed Jimmy was gay, she'd reject him, or at the very least, she would finally embrace Jake as her favorite son. Never mind that Jake was never able to come to his mother when she was in need. He was not reliable that way and he knew it. Jimmy, on the other hand, was never too busy to lend his mother a helping hand. This knowledge always made Jake angry.

Chapter 3

S ALLY ACKER GLANCED AT HER watch. *The taxi should be arriving in ten minutes,* she thought, surprised at the fleeting time. It was very pleasant sitting on her aunt's deck in Truro eating warm scones and drinking coffee as the sunrise fired across the sky, reflecting red in the calm bay waters.

On the way to Provincetown in the taxi, Sally's cell phone rang in her pocket. She retrieved it. It was the medical examiner. "Good morning, Stephanie."

"Say, listen, the guy with no ID yesterday turns out to be Arthur Milne, with a recent address on Court Street in Provincetown according to the Massachusetts Department of Motor Vehicles. He owns a 2010 silver Miata, license number MY-BABY. See if you can find it. On the other hand, we've had no luck so far locating a next of kin to validate the identity of the body."

"I'll get right on it."

"Good. I need you back here as soon as possible. We are crazy busy, and our backlog is getting worse." Stephanie hung up.

The taxi came over the crest of the road and descended the long hill, giving Sally a sprawling view of Provincetown; Pilgrim Monument, distinctive steeples, and beach houses cradled by the sea with massive dunes in the bright sunlight that framed the tiny town.

"*Wow!*" she gasped. *What a view,* Sally thought as the taxi glided closer to the town and turned onto Snail Road, then right to Commercial Street, and stayed right onto Bradford. At Standish Street, the taxi turned left to Lopes Square and wound its way along MacMillan Pier to the harbormaster's office, where it stopped. After paying the fare, Sally got out of the cab and walked to the office door, where the harbormaster, Burt Randell, appeared holding his gear, ready for a boat ride across the bay to the Long Point lighthouse.

"Beautiful day for traveling to the point," he told her, turned, and led the way to the patrol boat secured at the dock.

"Darn sight different from yesterday," Sally offered, following Burt to the patrol boat, where Provincetown's detective, Sylvia Santos, was waiting to join them.

Burt got on board, turned to help Sally and Sylvia onto the boat, and handed them each a life jacket before starting the engine of the vessel. He asked Sylvia to untie the two ropes holding the boat to the dock and carefully backed the boat out of its slip, positioning it facing out to the harbor and bay beyond. The morning air was warm and gentle against their faces, and quiet waters rippled into a V as the boat slowly cut through the water, creating only a very small wake.

Getting out of the patrol boat near the lighthouse entailed careful maneuvering of the stern of the boat into the shallow water near the beach. Sally took her shoes off before she disembarked from the vessel down a ladder into the shallow water, and with shoes tucked into her knapsack, she sloshed a short distance to the beach, followed by Sylvia.

"Thanks, Burt," Sally called back to the departing patrol boat. Burt waved and wished her well.

Sally surveyed the area as she sat in the warm sand while retrieving her shoes from her knapsack.

"I'll go look for evidence at the base of the lighthouse; I found the engraved watch there yesterday," Sally called to Sylvia, who had wandered toward the bunker to the west of where the body had lain.

"I'll give this an hour. I want to look more closely at the small wooden structure over there," Sylvia called over her shoulder.

The sun was intense, making the search challenging. The two investigators wore scooped baseball caps, sunglasses, and lightweight windbreakers over their T-shirts and jeans. Any worthy evidence they found was bagged, labeled, and placed into their knapsacks.

Sylvia found a part of a torn shirt stuck on the hut, probably snagged as someone passed by the rough wood of the building. She bagged it. She also added a single leather sandal to her collection of evidence, bagged it, labeled it, and put it into her knapsack. It was not clear yet if the leftovers they collected were evidence or just left behind by sun worshippers. It was wise to collect it now and sort it later.

"It's almost noon," Sally called to Sylvia. "It's time to start the trek back toward the moors and breakwater." Sally thought that it was nice to have someone working with her. "This can be a lonely job," she told Sylvia as they put their found objects into the knapsacks. Sylvia nodded her agreement.

"This afternoon we'll check out the Court Street apartment and talk to the neighbors," Sylvia told Sally.

"I'm looking forward to it."

Sally finished taking some pictures of the beach as she and Sylvia left the area of the small hut, remnants from a Civil War garrison. Sylvia told Sally that the locals referred to the Long Point Battery as Fort Useless.

"Interesting," Sally commented. They both smiled at the thought.

The walk back to the mainland was tranquil over the rocks that made up the jetty, and they passed several tourists on the way. Sally could never get used to the loss of life with no reason that she could understand. She sighed as she looked back over her shoulder at the beautiful beach that had held the terrible incident the day before. She stopped and scanned the horizon as if expecting some answers. She found none and moved on.

Chapter 4

NEIGHBORS KNOW THINGS IN A small town. This small town was like a big family—everyone knew something of the breaking story. Sylvia and Sally approached the Court Street address and met the landlord waiting for them. Sylvia had phoned him the evening before to set up the meeting.

Sylvia reached out her hand as she approached the landlord. "I'm Detective Santos, and this is Investigator Acker. Thank you for meeting us today," Sylvia said as she handed the landlord a search warrant for the condo.

"This is really a sad story," the landlord told them as he took the search warrant, read it, and unlocked the condo door for the detectives to enter.

A young man wearing a green T-shirt kneeling in the garden next to the victim's house strained to hear whatever he could from the exchanges between the detectives and the landlord.

The detectives entered the small condo, asking the landlord to wait at the door. Sally headed to the kitchen/living room area, while Sylvia headed to the bedroom and bathroom. Almost immediately, Sylvia found a pair of swim shorts and gold chain in the bureau drawer. She bagged the items and labeled the bags. Sylvia might not have noticed the items except that the shorts were clearly a different size from the other swim trunks in the drawer. The chain seemed out of place in the drawer, and that tweaked her interest. Otherwise the apartment seemed unusually tidy, as though it had been gone over and wiped clean. She brushed for fingerprints.

"Somebody knows how to clean up. I haven't found one fingerprint in this kitchen," Sally announced.

"The bathroom is spotless," Sylvia countered.

Taking bags of potential evidence, the two detectives left the condo and sealed the door with crime tape after the landlord locked it.

"Thank you. We may be in touch again," Sylvia told him as they turned away from the door and headed to the street, where a Provincetown Police car waited for them.

After placing the bags of evidence and equipment bag in the patrol car, they walked over to the young man next door tending his garden. As they approached, he stood up and smiled.

"Hi. I'm Sally Acker, with the state crime lab, and this is Detective Santos of the Provincetown Police Department. I'd like to ask you a few questions about two men who frequently stayed at this address. Are you familiar with what I'm talking about?"

"Is it related to the murder?" he asked.

"Yes, sorry to say that it is. Do you have any information for me, like a description of the men, your neighbor or the visitor?" she asked.

"Only that one came from New York, by the looks of his license plate. He drove a silver Cadillac SUV. I think that the other guy who lived here was a waiter in a restaurant on the waterfront. I think that's his Miata over there. Several times the police were called because of noise in the apartment."

Sylvia made a mental note to check the police log. As they prepared to leave, she called back to the police station to have the Miata impounded and sent to the state crime lab for testing.

"Do you think that you could describe the visitor to a police sketch artist?" she asked.

"Sure, I'd be glad to help," he answered.

At the police station, the young man wearing a green T-shirt worked with the police sketch artist to develop a sketch of the New York visitor. The drawing was circulated to police stations on Cape Cod and Albany, New York, with instructions to contact Detective Sylvia Santos with any information that could lead to his identification.

The day had gone well for Sally Acker. She was pleased that the neighbor was being so helpful. At 4:00 p.m. she headed back to the state lab to work on the autopsy report of the victim, identified as twenty-two-year-old Arthur Milne. His New York visitor's identity was just a matter of time.

****

Sylvia Santos and Barry "Bud" Black, the FBI agent on loan to the Provincetown Police Department, were getting acquainted in her office at the police station. She asked him a bit about his background experience in working murder cases. And Bud was responding. He had an extensive background in crime fighting and felt very comfortable with this new assignment, he told her. Drugs found on the victim and in his blood at the autopsy had cemented the FBI's involvement in the case, and they assigned Bud as their point man.

The entire Cape Cod Drug Task Force was now aware of the case and had offered any help they could give. Detective Santos was a member of the task force and privy to their database.

"We're grateful that the FBI could spare you to help us out. Their lab to process crime-scene evidence exceeds our capabilities. In the meantime, welcome aboard," Santos told Black.

"Hey, I'm glad to be here. Not every crime scene takes me to a resort as beautiful as this place," Bud said.

A phone call for Detective Santos interrupted the conversation.

"Excuse me. I have to take this call. Would you wait outside my office for a minute, please?" she asked him.

"No problem," he answered and left Detective Santos alone.

"Yes, ah ... hmm," Santos said several times while jotting down notes.

"Okay, Agent Black," she called. "Sorry for the interruption." She waved him back into the office and to a chair by her desk. Bud sauntered back into the office, sat down, slung his long arm over the back of the chair, and continued their discussion.

"Get any more leads on the murder at the lighthouse?" He leaned forward, eyeing the notes she had taken.

"There might be. We need someone to go to NYC to follow up on some interesting tips from Albany based on the police sketch we sent to them. Have you had any experience tracking persons of interest?"

He chuckled. "Why yes, I have. I spent some time with the international detective agency, RAID. I've tracked suspects in Mexico, Europe, and the states."

"I think that you could be of great help to us if you would follow up on these tips," Santos told Bud. He nodded in agreement.

"Right up my alley," he assured her. "Who will I talk with in the NYPD?"

"Guy Fox, captain at the central office of the NYPD. I'll let him know that you are coming. He'll be expecting you."

"I'll leave at dawn tomorrow. This is the kind of case I really like to get my teeth into." He stood, extending his hand to hers, and they shook hands. He turned toward the office door to exit. "I'll call you in the morning."

"We're counting on you, Bud. Thanks," Detective Santos told him. She was practical. Having the FBI involved might complicate things, but she was aware of the resources Agent Bud Black could call into play.

On his way out of the Provincetown police station, Bud felt a renewed sense of urgency. He knew that if you have no suspects in hours, the trail can easily grow cold. Cases like this took time, the very thing they did not have. This was far more complicated than he'd believed it was at first. Victim identity, motive, and perpetrator identity in a vast city like New York—all compounded the challenge. His phone vibrated in his pocket.

"Hello." Bud heard the voice of the FBI director, Sam Sturgess.

"Hi, Bud. Sam here. Just wanted to let you know that anything you need to solve this case is available. Just ask."

"Thanks. I'll be in touch," Bud told Sam, not knowing what he might need at this point in the investigation. His trip to speak with Guy Fox in New York City might shed some light on the mysteries evolving in this case. This would not be the first time he had met Guy Fox.

Chapter 5

BUD HAD COME FROM A long line of detectives. Both parents had made a career of combating crime. In his FBI training he had once tracked a drug smuggler through the Florida Everglades. Just like in the movies, he fought hand to hand to capture the criminal. Part of him found delight in the chase. Part of him, the rational part, thought the act too risky.

Bud had an impressive background in police work, highlighted by his FBI training. He remembered the conversation with his instructor at the academy when he completed his training with honors.

"Bud, not many officers finish this training at the high level of proficiency you have. I expect the FBI has plans for you," his instructor had told him.

"I'm ready, sir," Bud remembered answering.

It was true. The FBI had called him in for a conversation a few days after he had completed the program.

"Are you ready for your first official assignment in the real FBI world?" they asked him.

"Yes, sir. What is the assignment?" he had asked.

"You'll need to infiltrate a money-laundering scheme. It's dangerous. You'll be our eyes and ears. You'll set up the sting to bring them in," he had been told.

That was seven years ago, and Bud had had nothing but challenging FBI assignments. He had worked undercover, in disguise, and under a number of aliases. He most often used the alias Barry "Bud" Black, the highly respected agent at the Rosa Arroya International Detectives (RAID) office in Washington, DC. No matter what the assignment, Bud excelled.

The current case, a murder that may have been a crime of passion or a sex game gone wrong, would test his mind. There were limited clues: a pair of swim shorts, engraved watch, and gold chain, no apparent motive, and sketchy information from folks in the town. There was one sure thing: illegal drugs were found in the body.

One neighbor remembered a New York license plate and the last two numbers, an 8 and a 5, which could possibly pan out in the investigation. Also, the sketch sent to Albany had pointed the search to New York City. Mulling over the facts, Bud turned the key in his ignition to begin his five hour drive. He'd commence his search in New York City and meet with an old friend, Guy Fox, chief, NYPD.

Bud got started early when the traffic was light.

****

"Come in," Guy shouted as he rose from his desk and headed toward the door to welcome Bud.

"Good to see you again," Bud said as the two shook hands and hugged, with friendly backslapping.

"Sit. Let's talk," Guy said, pointing to one of two comfortable chairs positioned in front of his large desk strewn with case folders.

"I understand that you're working on a tough case. I've received the artist sketch from Albany, provided by Detective Santos at the Provincetown Police Department," Guy began.

"We have precious little to go on at this point," Bud confided.

"You have someone who remembers seeing a New York license plate, but only remembered the last two numbers?" Guy questioned.

"Right. That's why I'm here, as fruitless as it may be."

"Did they remember the make of the car?"

"He said it was a silver Cadillac SUV. Looked new and shiny."

"Well, that's something. You can go through our database and see what you can find. Even a police warning on a simple traffic violation will put a license number into our database," Guy divulged.

Bud settled himself into a small detective's room at the NYPD and began his search on their computer.

First, he isolated all New York license plate numbers ending in 85. Even this was iffy, based on an unsure neighbor's memory. Ten thousand numbers ending in 85 popped up on the screen.

Second, on a hunch, he isolated all silver Cadillac SUVs built in the last three years. The search narrowed to five hundred names in the area.

He then isolated the city vehicle tags from other areas in New York State.

This approach produced a huge amount of information for Bud to sort through. He sorted the findings by grouping the vehicles by silver color, luxury SUV, and the 85, the last two numbers on the license. This helped to cull out of the massive findings a more manageable data set of ninety names.

After two hours of work, Bud took a coffee break and stretched his legs. His mind continued to go over and over the few details he had. He remembered the neighbor saying that the visitor from New York was good-looking, wore expensive clothes, and visited on weekends. This profile led Bud to suspect that the visitor might be single, or if he was married, the guy had money. Tracking down the car and the owner was Bud's priority.

Finishing his coffee and clearing his head, Bud returned to work sifting through possible connections to the mystery car.

****

On the second day, Guy stopped by the detective's room to check on Bud's progress.

"How's it going?" Guy inquired.

"Slow, but I've made some progress. I've narrowed the list to ninety names. The really good news is that five names look very promising," Bud told the chief.

"Super! Say, I wanted to tell you that Rosa Arroya is coming to New York City for a visit. She'll arrive tomorrow. If you're free, we'll all go out to dinner," he told Bud.

"I'd love to. I've missed her since I've been out of the RAID office these last seven months. I can hardly wait to catch up. Where are we going? What time will we meet?"

"Whoa! Slow down. We'll decide when she gets here tomorrow," Guy answered.

"Got it!" Bud acknowledged the plan and went back to work. But tomorrow couldn't come fast enough for Bud to reconnect with his RAID boss and personal friend, Rosa.

As Bud prepared to close up for the day, he took one last glance at his puzzle. He had been able to narrow his search to two dozen matches—silver Cadillac SUV in the city with license plates ending in 85. He had run detailed information on the owners of the vehicles. Were they married or single men or women? In what part of the city did they live? He had made a list of those hits that matched the categories.

1. George Mendez – Bronx, NY
2. Richard Andrews – Manhattan, NYC
3. Paul Spinoza – Brooklyn, NY
4. Saul Greenburg – Manhattan, NYC
5. Jake Dimmer – Manhattan, NYC

Bud eliminated George Mendez and Paul Spinoza from the first batch of potential suspects because their addresses were out of Manhattan. The three remaining names were in the city, and he planned to go to each address, find the car, and find the owner for questioning. Bud locked the room, filed his research findings in the desk drawer, and headed out to his car with printout in hand of the three remaining names and addresses.

The first residence on his list was that of Richard Andrews.

As Bud drove up to the Andrews address near Mimi Towers, he spotted a Silver Cadillac SUV parked on the street in a handicapped space. Its license plate ended in 85. He parked nearby for a few minutes and took pictures of the car and its full license plate. Just as he decided to go to the address, he saw a young woman assisting an older man on a walker to the SUV. After helping the man into the passenger's side of the car, the woman slid behind the wheel and drove away. Bud jotted down on his notepad next to Andrews—*low priority*.

The next name on Bud's list was Saul Greenburg. His address was a well-maintained high-rise on West Sixty-Eighth Street across from Central Park, with underground parking. Bud pulled up to the reserved space in front of the high-rise entrance. The doorman came immediately to the car as Bud opened the passenger side window and flashed his FBI identification.

"Can I be of assistance, sir?" the doorman asked Bud.

"Yes. Can you tell me if the Greenburgs are residing here?" Bud asked the smartly dressed doorman.

"Well, sir, they do have a residence here, but they only use it from April to July. They reside the rest of the months in Paris, France. They will be back next spring, I believe."

"Does anyone use the car while they are away?" Bud wanted to know.

"No, sir."

"Thank you for your time. You've been very helpful," Bud told the doorman. Based on this information, he decided that this car was not of value in his search. He made a note next to Greenburg—*low priority*.

The third Manhattan, NYC, address was that of Jake Dimmer, who owned a condo up on the Hudson in New York. The Dimmer address was in a very high-end area of the Upper East Side, off Fifth Avenue and Sixtieth Street. Bud pulled up in front of the address and was greeted by the doorman.

"Can I help you, sir?" the doorman asked, leaning down and speaking through the open passenger side window of the car.

Bud flashed his FBI identification and asked, "Is Mr. Dimmer in residence?"

"Why, yes, sir. He just returned home late last night from a business trip," the doorman explained.

"Where does he park his car?" Bud asked the doorman, still bending over at the car window.

"We park his car in our garage for him, sir."

"It would be a big help if you would get in the car and take me to Mr. Dimmer's car," Bud told the doorman.

"Of course, sir." He hesitated for a moment, opened the car door, and slid in next to Bud in the front seat.

The garage door was controlled by a remote held in the doorman's hand. Bud drove following the doorman's directions into the secured garage. He drove to a parked silver Cadillac SUV at the end of a long row of neatly polished Porsches, BMWs, and Lexus'. Bud stopped, got out of the car, and took pictures at all angles of the SUV, including the full license plate, MAN-1585.

"What can you tell me about Mr. Dimmer?" Bud asked the doorman as he got back into the car.

"He is very wealthy. He married Cathy Astor, a New York debutante from Scarsdale, New York, about three years ago. They also have a place in the Hamptons. She walks their standard poodle every morning around eleven. He travels a lot and rarely talks with anyone," answered the doorman, who prided himself on knowing everything about everyone he served.

"Thank you. You have been very helpful," Bud told the doorman, and they drove out of the garage and back to the doorman's station at the building's entrance.

"Is there anything else I can do for you, sir?" the doorman asked politely as he got out of the car.

"Not now, thank you," Bud answered. As Bud pulled away into traffic, he could see the doorman shrug his shoulders and shake his head trying to make sense of it all.

Bud marked a big star next to Jake Dimmer's name and wrote—*promising*!

His instincts told him that he was on the right track. Now it was time for dinner at Bud's favorite pizza joint.

****

Bud was up bright and early. He had decided to go to the NYPD office and research as much as he could find on Jake Dimmer and his wife. He made his way to the chief's office with his request to access personal data on Mr. Dimmer.

"Sounds like a breakthrough," Guy told him as he led him to a resource room. They sat down in front of a computer, and the chief entered his password.

"All yours," he told Bud as he rose to leave.

"Thanks. Hey, what time are we on tonight for dinner with Rosa?" Guy smiled and raised six fingers. "Meet in my office."

Bud felt a wave of joy and excitement sweep over him at the thought of an evening visit and reminiscing with Rosa, his best friend. They knew each other well and had shared many crime-solving experiences together. She was a very special friend to him.

He returned his thoughts to Mr. Dimmer as he tapped the name into the search bar on the computer. It seemed like only an instant, and then the screen filled with codes related to Jake Dimmer. Bud thought that the FBI was the only agency with such equipment. *I guess not*, he thought as the page of information appeared following Jake Dimmer's name in bold.

A thirty-five-year-old salesman, recently married to debutante Cathy Astor, residing in Upper East Side apartment rented to him and belonging to the Astor family. NOTE: Questions remain in FBI files regarding his substantial wealth considering his lack of an advanced degree or training in a trade, and a questionable history of employment declared on his tax returns. The subject remains on a watch list based on his frequent trips to the Cayman Islands and suspected drug trafficking.

Bud was even more convinced that this information could fit his profile of the suspect. He decided to talk with Dimmer's wife this morning at eleven while she walked the dog, before talking with Jake.

In preparation for meeting Mrs. Dimmer, Bud researched her background. Somehow, she was so much more polished and experienced in her life of successes and awards than Jake could claim. *This guy must be some charmer.* Mrs. Cathy Astor Dimmer was involved in every charitable cause you could think of: the American Cancer Society, Society for the Prevention of Cruelty to Animals, Soup Kitchens of New York, and the arts, theater, and symphony boards. Her charitable donations added up to well over $500,000 a year. *Seems like Jake may be one of her charities*, Bud thought as he continued to read about Cathy's life.

It was a perfect day for a walk in the park. Bud timed his arrival to the area where Cathy Dimmer walked her poodle every morning according to what the doorman had said. He found a bench near the entrance closest to the Dimmer home. It was almost eleven when he saw a woman in a navy blue running suit walking a silver standard poodle. The two were headed his way and would soon pass by the bench. Bud caught her eye as she passed by.

"Hello, Cathy," he said.

The woman turned toward Bud. "Do I know you?" she asked.

"No. My name is Barry 'Bud' Black, and I'm with the FBI," he told her and stood as he showed her his identification.

"Oh? Am I in trouble?" she asked as one would who had nothing to fear. She was tall and had a gracious air about her, very well-groomed, and made direct eye contact with Bud.

"Mrs. Dimmer, I hope that you will answer a few questions about your husband, Jake, for me," Bud told her.

"Jake? Is he in some kind of trouble?" Her eyes moved to the poodle and away from Bud's face.

"I just need to know what his travel schedule has been over the last six months. Could you tell me that?" Bud asked, watching for signs of discomfort.

"I'm not sure that I should be talking to you." She hesitated. "Then you already know that he travels extensively for his work in sales," she responded with a bit of an edge, looking directly into Bud's eyes again.

"What does he sell?"

"I really don't know. I never asked. You should talk with Jake directly, not to me," she answered, showing a bit of irritation.

"Surely you must have wondered about his excessive spending on expensive cars, condos, and travel," Bud pushed.

"Not really. He has his life and I have mine," she said dismissively.

"Can you explain what you mean?" Bud asked as Cathy and the dog began to move back the way they had come. Bud walked beside her in silence for a while.

Cathy broke the silence. "I am and always have been involved with many charities, art museums, hospitals, and fund-raising events. I am very busy. When Jake is home, he joins me. Why all these questions?"

"Do you know where Jake was last week?" Bud probed, trying not to push too hard.

"Business in Philadelphia," she told Bud.

"He told you that?"

"Yes."

"Did you believe him?" Bud saw a look cross Cathy's face that belied her doubt.

In her own mind, Cathy was troubled by the last year with Jake's extended and frequent trips. She suspected another woman, but had not yet confronted the issue. She did not respond to Bud's question.

"I will not answer any more questions about my husband. Ask him yourself," she snapped.

"Is Jake home now?"

"Yes. We're planning a Cayman Islands getaway."

"When do you leave?"

"Soon. Talk to my husband," she told him as she walked her silver poodle toward the door to her home.

"Who minds your dog?" Bud asked.

"Talk to my husband. Good-bye," she told him and entered the door to the building. Bud put his foot in the door to stop it from closing.

"Cathy, please let me talk to your husband now," he asked, showing her his FBI identification again.

The three—Cathy Dimmer, the standard poodle, and Bud Black—got onto the elevator headed for the Dimmer's penthouse apartment. It was a fast ride to the private entrance to the apartment. Cathy, still holding her elevator key and leashed dog, stepped into the hall of the apartment when the elevator door opened.

"Jake, I'm home," she called. "There is someone here to talk with you," she continued loudly as she unclipped the dog's leash and hung it on a hook. The elevator door closed silently behind them.

"You can wait here," she motioned to Bud as she pointed to the tastefully furnished living room.

Bud chose to stand as Cathy, followed by the poodle, went to look for Jake. Bud heard her call "Jake" again on her way. His eyes scanned the room for pictures, books, or computer. The room was void of any sign of interests or hobbies, not even a wedding picture above the fireplace.

"Hi, honey. You called?" Jake said, coming from his study to meet Cathy in the hall not far from the living room.

"Yes. An FBI agent is waiting in the living room to talk to you," Cathy told him as he embraced her and gave her a kiss on the cheek.

"FBI?" Jake was noticeably shaken. "What does he want with me?" he asked her, holding her at arm's length.

"Something about your travel schedule over the past few months, I think," Cathy told him, stepping back from his embrace. "Was there trouble?"

Jake began to sweat as he walked toward the living room where Bud waited. As Jake entered the room, Bud moved toward Jake, hand extended showing his FBI identification as he introduced himself.

"Mr. Dimmer, my name is Bud Black of the FBI. I'm here to ask you a few questions. Is that okay with you?"

Jake fought to stay calm and cooperative, so that he would not appear suspicious to the agent. His pulse rate quickened.

"I guess so," Jake answered nervously.

"Can I call you Jake?" Bud asked.

"Yeah, I suppose so," he stammered, trying to remain cool.

"Jake, where were you last week between Thursday and Sunday?"

Jake's mind flashed back to Provincetown. "Philadelphia," he answered, almost too quickly, as he glanced out of the window with his back to Bud.

"What were you doing in Philadelphia?"

"It was a business trip," Jake answered, still not looking at Bud.

"What kind of business?"

This was the question Jake had prepared to answer whenever it was asked and by whoever asked it. "It is top-secret work for an international company headquartered in Philadelphia," he answered, exuding confidence, like a child telling a convincing lie.

"Does the company have a name?" Bud pushed.

Jake began to sweat more heavily and fidget with coins in his pants pocket. He reached for his hanging suit jacket by the door to retrieve his faux business cards. It was all part of his charade and secret life.

"Here." Jake handed Bud a glossy business card.

Jake Dimmer, Vice President
Private Investigations
Global, LTD
c/o P.O. Box 400
New York, NY 10012

"Do you have a telephone number for a client to reach you?" Bud asked Jake.

"No. All requests for services must be in writing. I take the requests to Global," Jake answered, sinking deeper and deeper into his make-believe world.

"Who can I talk to at Global to verify your employment with them?" Bud asked, holding a small notepad to record needed information.

"They won't admit to my existence. I work undercover, and the work is top-secret," Jake continued his story.

Bud decided to change the direction of his questions. "Have you ever had work on Cape Cod?"

Jake felt the heat of the question, and it made him very uncomfortable. He thought quickly that it might be a trap. This was the time to implicate his brother.

"No. The only time I've been to Cape Cod was when I drove my brother there one weekend a couple of months ago. He loves the cape and goes to Provincetown as often as he can find the time," Jake lied. It was just like when they were kids. Jake would lie; Jim, his twin, would take the rap.

Bud was not prepared for this twist. "Your brother?" he asked.

"Yeah. I have an identical twin brother named Jim. He is a dental surgeon in New York City. I haven't seen him for quite some time, considering my travel schedule. I don't exactly support his lifestyle. Actually, he watches the dog when we need him," Jake continued, lying and weaving more doubt toward his twin brother.

"Will Jim stay here to mind the dog when you and Mrs. Dimmer go off to the Cayman Islands? When was that, next week?" Bud asked.

This caught Jake off guard. "Yes. How did you know that?" Jake asked, noticing that the FBI agent was now interested in Jim.

"That's not important. What is important is that I speak with your brother," Bud told him.

"The trip is next week. Why not come by Thursday? We'll be gone, and Jim will be here after his office hours around three in the afternoon." Jake was very pleased with himself. The story was going the way he had planned if ever he had to defend himself. "I really must continue packing and making final arrangements for our trip. Is there anything else you need from me?" Jake said, gesturing toward the door and elevator.

"No. Thank you. I can see myself out," Bud said, getting into the elevator that Jake had called. "Thank you for your time. Enjoy the Cayman Islands," he told him as the door closed and the elevator began its descent.

On his way down from the penthouse, Bud felt conflicted with the new information from Jake. There were too many loose ends in Jake's story, and this twist of a twin brother didn't help anything. Bud's gut told him that Jake was his man, but proving it would be another story. He needed to talk with Dr. Dimmer as soon as possible.

Bud glanced at his watch to see that it was just after two thirty in the afternoon. He had time to Google Dr. James Dimmer and go to his office near Times Square. On his way to the dentist's office, Bud telephoned Guy.

"Hello, Guy? I need a favor."

"What can I do for you?" asked Guy.

"I'm on my way to Dr. Dimmer's dental office near Times Square. He is the identical twin of Jake Dimmer, my suspect. Can you send two officers there? I want him brought in for questioning in the lighthouse murder," Bud told Guy. "I've run into an unexpected twist in the case. I need to put pressure on both Dr. Dimmer and his twin," Bud explained.

"Is Dr. Dimmer our man?" Guy asked.

"No. I need you to play along with me on this one. My suspect, Jake, just threw his brother under the bus."

"Are you sure?"

"I'm as sure as I can be at this point in the investigation. I want to lay a trap, but it will depend on Dr. Dimmer's cooperation once he understands what is going on."

"Okay, but only because it's you asking for this favor. Don't forget how the NYPD cooperated with the FBI!" Guy rubbed it in.

They both got a laugh out of that idea, and the call ended.

****

They brought James Dimmer, DDS, in for questioning. He asked for a lawyer right away. The questioning was rescheduled for the next day.

The day had flown by. When Bud glanced at his watch, his mind registered—dinnertime!

Bud walked toward the chief's office. As he rounded the corner in the hallway, he spotted Rosa Arroya looking in his direction. They walked quickly toward each other, arms wide-open for a big bear hug.

"Rosa, it's so good to see you," he whispered into her ear.

"Oh, Bud, it's good to see you too," Rosa responded. "How are you?"

"I'm fine. Busy. I'm hoping to return to RAID soon. But you know that," he blurted out.

"Hey, you two," called Guy. "Let's get out of here. The workday is over."

"You must be kidding. When is the workday over for you?" Rosa called back.

The three, arm in arm, walked out of the police station and onto the busy New York City streets for a night of good food, reminiscing about old times and cases they had all shared, and being together as good friends enjoy doing.

Chapter 6

I N THE INTERROGATION ROOM, THE NYPD captain, Guy Fox, FBI
agent Bud Black, and Dr. Dimmer's attorney, Barry Silversmith,
listened to James Dimmer speak.

"I'm sure this is all a misunderstanding. I'm not really sure why
I'm here in the first place. From what Agent Black told me, you already
know about my childhood in a project in NYC, my struggles with a
bullying twin brother, and my ultimate success as a dental surgeon,"
he told them. "What is it you want to know?" There seemed to be a
momentary feeling of trust. Then Bud asked the first question.

"What were you doing in Provincetown last weekend, the day of
the murder?" he was asked.

"What murder?" he answered in shock.

"Mr. Dimmer, we ask the questions," Bud reminded him.

"I went with my brother. He was driving and I hitched a ride with
him. I wanted to go on a whale watch," he answered.

"Do you have a car?" Bud asked.

"No. I find that I can get where I want to go by public transportation
most of the time," he answered.

"What kind of car does your brother have?"

"I think it's a silver Cadillac SUV," he answered.

"What time did you arrive? Where did he drop you off?"

"It was morning in time for the eleven o'clock whale watch. He
dropped me off at the pier."

"Were you supposed to meet later?"

"Yes, but he never showed up."

"What was he going to do while you were on the whale watch?"

"He said he was meeting with a client for business."

"What kind of business?"

"I don't know. He never talked about his work."

"Where were they to meet?"

"He didn't say."

"How did your swim trunks and gold chain get into the victim's apartment?" Bud probed, showing Jim pictures of the evidence, including an engraved watch, "*Love, J.D.*," found at the crime scene. He looked surprised at the pictures, remembering that Jake had suggested he leave the items in the glove compartment that day.

"I don't know. I was never at an apartment in Provincetown that day or any day. I took the bus back to New York; I didn't stay overnight. I have never seen that watch. It's not mine," he explained.

"Do you have any thought on how your swim trunks were found at the victim's apartment?" Guy continued.

"No. I have never been in trouble with the law. I don't know who the victim is. Was it a man or a woman?" he asked, showing signs of fatigue.

"A man. You don't deny that the items we have shown you are yours?"

"As far as I can tell in the pictures, the items may be mine. I have no idea how they got there. The last I saw them was when I put them in the glove compartment in my brother's car. I don't date men," he insisted.

"Interesting!" Bud murmured.

Dr. Dimmer's attorney spoke. "He said the watch wasn't his. What else do you have?"

"You can see in the photos the swim trunks, watch, and gold chain," Bud said, pointing to each item as he spoke. He turned to James Dimmer. "So you deny knowing the victim, Mr. Milne?"

"That's right. I do not know any Mr. Milne. I had nothing to do with this crime." Jim was emphatic. "I didn't leave anything. I wasn't there!"

"So let me get this right. You admit that these could be your things, refuse to admit that you were at the apartment where we found these items, and state that you got to Provincetown with your twin brother—who, by the way, has denied even going to Provincetown, let alone driving you there! He says that he was in Philadelphia on business," Bud told him.

"He's lying!" Jim blurted out without thinking.

"Why would he lie?"

"I don't know. When we were kids, he'd lie, and I'd take the punishment for something he did," he told Bud.

"So you think that your brother is lying?"

"I only know that we were both in Provincetown last weekend," he insisted. "We had nothing to do with a murder!"

"You said that you were not with your brother that day after you got to town. How do you know what he did that day, considering he says he wasn't even there?" Bud pressed.

Suddenly Jim turned to his attorney, saw him shake his head, and stopped sharing anything. It dawned on him that this was serious. In total frustration, Jimmy put his forehead down on his folded arms on the table and fell silent.

The attorney, Barry Silversmith, put his hand on Jimmy's shoulder and announced, "We're done here, unless you are going to charge my client."

After a silent pause, Bud nodded to the attorney that they could go. "Don't leave town. We'll want to talk to you again," Bud reminded Jimmy.

The attorney ushered his client out of the interrogation room.

Guy and Bud looked at each other.

Bud said, "I can't say that I've ever had a case like this one—identical twins pointing at each other. I believe Jimmy. But how will I snare Jake? I think that Jake is our man! He had access to the items in his glove compartment and could have planted them."

"Are you saying that Jake swings both ways, considering the murder evidence is pointing to a gay sex game gone wrong?" Guy asked.

"I need to find out. Things may not be as they seem between Mr. and Mrs. Dimmer. Furthermore, Jim's story doesn't make sense as long as his brother holds to the story that he was in Philadelphia and not in Provincetown. I'm ready to find out where Jake really was," Bud said forcefully.

"I like the idea. We haven't pressed his alibi, and it is now time to clear up a few things," Guy answered as they headed to the computer desk to scour their records for more information on the brother, Jake Dimmer, and Global, LTD. "Why don't I check out Dr. Dimmer while we are at it?" Guy suggested.

"Good idea," Bud agreed. "Did anyone see the silver Cadillac SUV that morning in town? Did anyone remember our whale-watcher on board that morning? I'll follow up on these questions in Provincetown," Bud told Guy, eager to track the leads.

"Go for it." Guy said. "Remember, the NYPD is here and ready to help. Just say the word."

The two left the station, hell-bent on finding the truth.

****

Later that night, Bud sent a coded message
on his RAID smart pen to Rosa.

"Need to talk—call me."

Bud was on loan to the FBI from RAID, and he always carried his RAID pen so he could touch base with Rosa. Having had dinner with Guy and Rosa in New York was very special. The three of them had talked about their challenges in their most recent case, Priority #1. Rosa and he had solved many crimes over the years. They worked well together. He needed to talk to her.

It was just before midnight when Bud's hotel room phone rang. "Hello."

"Bud, its Rosa. What's up? I got your message," she told him.

"I need to brainstorm with you about this case I mentioned to you the other night at dinner," he told her.

"You're in luck. I have some time. As a matter of fact, I have a week's vacation coming up," she said joyfully.

"That's great, a busman's holiday. Do you mind?" Bud asked.

"Not at all. Will you be in New York, or are you going to return to Provincetown?" she asked.

"I need to get back to Provincetown, but I can stay an extra day in New York if that would be better for you," he told her.

"Nonsense, I'll come to Provincetown for vacation! When are you heading back to the cape?" she asked him.

"I'll be back there by Friday of this week," he answered.

"I can take a morning flight from DC to Boston, giving me time to get the ferry in Boston. Do you have any idea where I can stay in Provincetown?"

"The Provincetown Police Department and the FBI have arranged for me to stay in a two-bedroom waterfront condo while I'm working on this case. You can stay with me," he told her.

"Fine. I'll contact you from the ferry on my way into Provincetown," she said.

"Great, I'll meet you at the pier," Bud answered. "Rosa"—he paused—"thank you!"

"Good night," she said warmly and hung up.

Bud felt a calm come over him, because working with Rosa added another dimension to the crime-solving team. They fit like a hand to a glove, he thought. He turned out the bedside lamp and fell into a deep sleep.

Chapter 7

In Attorney Silversmith's office, Jimmy tried to grasp how serious this accusation by his brother was for him.

"This is not kid's stuff, Jim. This is murder!" Silversmith yelled.

"I know. I know," the flustered young man responded. "But what can I do? It's his word against mine. And history tells me that I will lose."

"Not this time, Jimmy. Not this time," Barry Silversmith said firmly. "We need to mount a full-scale investigation into your brother's whereabouts last weekend. Are you with me?" the attorney asked as he brought two cups of coffee to the table.

There was a long silence as Jimmy contemplated the suggestion. What if Jake was guilty of this crime? What if Jake was gay? What about Cathy in all of this? Did he really want to go down this road? On the other hand, did he want to go to jail for a death he was not responsible for and had no part in? Maybe it was time to put the blame where it belonged. At least an investigation could clear them of any wrongdoing.

"Yes, we need an investigation to clear our names," Jimmy answered.

"You do realize that it may clear your name. There is no guarantee that it will clear Jake's name," his attorney reminded him.

"Of course it will. Jake isn't a monster. He's no killer. He's not even gay," Jimmy insisted. "It could have been an accident. I'm innocent and so is Jake!"

"We'll see. Are you giving me the go-ahead to mount a full-scale investigation then?" Attorney Silversmith asked.

Jimmy swallowed hard, wiped sweat from his brow with the napkin that came with the coffee he hadn't touched, and nodded. "Yes."

"Jimmy, sign this agreement for the investigation," Barry said, pushing a paper in front of Jimmy and handing him a pen.

Jimmy picked up the paper and read what he was agreeing to, then put it down on the desk and signed it.

"You won't regret this. It is high time that you stand up for yourself. You are innocent!" Silversmith told him emphatically. The attorney believed Jimmy was innocent. He saw the confusion in his eyes on the first day he had been brought in for questioning. He had been working with this family for years and had seen the disparity between the boys, now men. He would not see this end poorly for Jim. A wave of righteousness overcame him as he slipped the signed contract into his briefcase. It wasn't right, and he would prove it!

They shook hands and ended their meeting. Jimmy walked out of the office feeling both relieved and guilty at what he had just done.

The minute Jimmy Dimmer left the office, Barry phoned his friend, a private investigator, Burt Brambly, of *Surveillance Is Our Business, Inc.* (S.O.B.) for the job.

Chapter 8

CATHY DIMMER HAD A FEW more days to prepare for their trip to the Cayman Islands. Bud's visit while walking her dog had unsettled her. She needed some answers to the nagging question "Is Jake having an affair?"

"Hi, sis. I need to talk. Can we meet for a drink today?" Cathy asked her sister, Carole, her best friend and confidante.

"Of course. What's up?" her sister asked.

"Can you come now?" Cathy blurted out.

Sensing that this was an emergency, Carole answered, "Yes. I'll come get you in the Porsche. Meet me at the front door in fifteen."

Cathy felt relieved. Jake was away for the day, on business he said, and she felt free.

Cathy grabbed her Italian leather shoulder bag and left the penthouse through the elevator to the lobby and the front door. The flashy black Porsche pulled up as the doorman opened the door for her. She waved to her sister Carole, who was driving, and rushed to get into the convertible.

They headed to a spot they both knew at the water's edge, the Fish Bar.

The owner, standing behind the bar polishing glasses, yelled hi to the women as they entered. "The usual wine?" he called.

"No. Two gin and tonics," Cathy answered.

"Oh, need something for your nerves, eh?" the owner questioned. "Coming up!"

Cathy and her sister settled at a small corner table outside on the patio under a colorful umbrella.

"Tell me what's going on," Carole said.

When the drinks arrived, Cathy gulped hers down as though it was water and motioned to the owner for another. She felt the alcohol take hold as she turned to her sister and spoke.

"Sis, I'm beside myself with suspicion. I think that Jake is having an affair. He may also be mixed up in a crime of some sort," she told her sister in one big exhale.

"Oh, my God!" Carole gasped. "I don't believe it!"

"The FBI came to question me, and then they questioned Jake."

"What did they ask about?"

"They wanted to know about Jake's travel schedule. Frankly, so do I!" Cathy swirled down her second gin and tonic.

"Do you think Jake is lying to you?"

"I think that he has a mistress!" Cathy explained with a mix of hurt and anger in her voice. "He is staying away more often for longer periods of time. When he returns home, he is overly thoughtful and attentive, maybe out of guilt. He has begun to use a new aftershave lotion. I think that he is in love."

"Can you be sure? Did you confront him about it?"

"No, but my instincts tell me that something is very wrong," Cathy told her sister.

"You need to have him followed. You need to have proof that he is cheating!"

"We are going on a last-minute vacation to the Cayman Islands in a few days. Jake hastily made all the arrangements, and now I have to rearrange my schedule. I'm not even sure that I want to go with him," she told her sister.

"Cathy, do you have a will? A prenup?" her sister asked.

"What do you mean?"

"I just watched a crime story where the husband kills the wife for her money and then runs away with his mistress. Why not tell him that you just can't go? You don't have enough time to reschedule ..."

Before Carole could finish her thought, Cathy grabbed her hand and held it tight. "What are you saying?" Cathy's suspicion of her husband's affair was dulled by her sister's question, "Do you have a will, a prenup?" Cathy glanced at her wristwatch.

Carole gently released her hand from Cathy's grip. "I'm just saying that you need some answers, that's all."

"I need to get back to the flat. I'll call you later. I need to think," Cathy told her sister. But almost instantly, Cathy had a change of heart about going home. They hugged, and after paying the bill, walked to the car.

"You can count on me. You know that, don't you?" Carole whispered.

"I know I can." Cathy's mind was whirling with frightening thoughts. *What if he wants to kill me to be with his mistress?* She began to sweat, and her mouth became very dry.

"Can I use your cell phone?" Cathy asked her sister after getting into the car.

Carole handed her the cell phone and started the car.

"Hello, Roger. I need to talk with you now. Call 212-345-6789, my sister's cell," she said to an answering machine at their family lawyer's office, Roger Milburne Associates.

"Drive me to his office," she told her sister. His office was just eight New York blocks away.

Traffic was moderate at that time of day, so they were able to get to the office in record time. As they pulled into a parking spot, the cell phone rang. Cathy answered.

"Hello. Hi, Roger. Thanks for responding so quickly. I need to see you right now. I'm outside of your office. Where are you?" Cathy said in one breath. She listened. "Great; we're coming up."

He was at the door to meet the sisters when they arrived.

Roger had a spacious office, furnished with a mahogany desk, a conference table, and comfortable chairs. Behind his desk was a bookcase filled with appropriate law books. Van Gogh's *Starry Night* and several paintings of Picasso's blue period hung on his walls. It spoke of his success.

"Well, it is always good to see you, but I sense that this is not a pleasure visit," he said, noting Cathy's stressed look. He led them to his office with his arm around Cathy's shoulders.

"Roger, I'm a mess. I think Jake is having an affair," she stammered.

"What makes you think that?" he asked her.

"The FBI came to our flat to question me and then Jake about his travel schedule. I think he is involved in some kind of crime."

"That's not good. Have you had him followed? Do you have any proof?" Roger asked.

"No. But I will. He may be planning to kill me," she said breathlessly.

"What?"

"He wants me to take a hastily planned trip in a few days to the Cayman Islands. I'm afraid. I don't want to go."

"Your will, considering that you refused a prenup, leaves him everything. Maybe we need to change that today," Roger offered. "Let's secure your assets into a trust, restricting access and structuring it for you and your children," he suggested.

"I don't have any children," Cathy responded.

"You will one day. This is precautionary," he told her.

"Can this be in place soon?" Cathy asked.

"Yes, you'll sign the document, and I'll notarize it before you leave. It will be ready tomorrow. Most of the trust is structured to comply with the law. The personalized pages that will be included will specify exactly how your personal assets will be held in trust for your children and you in the event of a divorce or your distribution wishes in the event of your untimely death. It will specify that Jake will be excluded from your personal assets."

"I don't want to go with him," Cathy repeated. "I feel afraid."

"Then don't go. Tell him you have something that cannot be rearranged."

"That's what I suggested," added Carole.

"Thank you, Roger. You've been such a good friend to the family and to me," she said, promising to return the next day to read the trust document and to sign it.

Cathy and her sister left the law office feeling calmer now that they had done something. Next they needed to find a private eye and get him on the case immediately.

Carole took hold of Cathy's arm. "My neighbor hired a private eye."

"Did it work out okay?" Cathy asked her sister.

"It worked out just fine. They used *Surveillance Is Our Business, Inc.*," Carole told her as she tapped in the company name to the GPS before starting the car and following the directions to the S.O.B. office.

A sign in front of a small, shabby office building said *Surveillance Is Our Business, Inc.* They parked the car on the street in front of the entrance door to the office. Both of the women entered the door into a shabby office, strewn with boxes and case folders on the floor. The place smelled of cigars.

"Can I help you?" said the overly made-up young receptionist, speaking from behind a table desk. Her false eyelashes, bright red lipstick, and big brown eyes were the only bright spots in the drab office space.

"I'm not sure. By 'Surveillance,' do you mean undercover work?" Cathy asked tentatively.

"That's what it means, and no one does it better!" the receptionist answered, snapping her gum.

"Then you can help me."

"Agent Brambly will be back in ten minutes. In the meantime, here is a form to fill out to get things rolling," the receptionist said, handing Cathy a clipboard, form, and pen.

Cathy and her sister sat on two wooden chairs placed against the wall next to the door. The form had the usual questions—name, address, telephone number, and the reason for the needed company services. The last question jumped out at Cathy; she was actually going to accuse her husband of cheating, with no proof but a gut feeling.

"Is this all kept confidential?" Cathy called to the receptionist from where she was seated.

"Absolutely! We wouldn't be in business very long if we blabbed everything. You can trust us. Not to worry," she responded from across the room, snapping her gum again and again. Cathy was relieved that no one else was in the waiting area.

At that moment, Agent Burt Brambly came into the office through the front door. He was a large man, with mousey brown and gray curly hair and sleepy green eyes. He wore a loosely fitting suede jacket with bulging pockets over a baggy pair of jeans. After a wave to the receptionist, who pointed to the guests, he turned to address Cathy and her sister.

"Trouble in paradise?" he asked.

Cathy took an immediate dislike to the man and wondered if she should proceed. But fear overshadowed her gut-level feelings about the man towering before her reaching for the clipboard and form she held.

"Maybe," she answered with a knot in her stomach, while giving Mr. Brambly the clipboard.

It was a shame that he was so rude, considering he exuded confidence, and in some ways, was an appealing guy.

"May I call you Cathy?" he asked.

"I prefer Mrs. Dimmer," she snapped.

"Of course. Please come into my office, where we can talk candidly, Mrs. Dimmer," he told Cathy and her sister. "And this is?" he asked, holding his hand out to Carole.

"Carole Avery, my sister," Cathy responded.

They all moved to a small, air-conditioned office, and sat down at a small table.

"Mrs. Dimmer, I want to be frank with you. I charge $300 per day, plus expenses to include videotape and photo development, travel, and communication. I'll work tirelessly for you, and I will prove without a doubt that your suspicions about your husband are right or wrong. I can usually tie up a case like this in less than thirty days. Do you understand me?" he asked.

Cathy was stunned by the expense at first, but then realized she could be talking about her own life, never mind the existence of a mistress. "Yes, I understand. How do we begin?"

"How do you want me to proceed? Confront him? Track him? Befriend him? Or go about my business gathering information to answer your question of his infidelity?"

Cathy thought for a moment. "You need to shadow him wherever he goes, including a trip to the Cayman Islands in a few days. He wants me to go, but frankly I'm concerned for my safety," she confessed. She was beginning to soften a bit toward the straight-talking, burly guy.

"So, money is no object for you, I gather," he stated after hearing his assignment.

"I'll tell you when the till is empty. Until then, you have up to thirty days to report to me on who this man is that I have married."

"Okay. I'll need a retainer to get moving on this," he told her.

"How much?" she asked with no expectations.

"The least this will cost you is $9,000. Fifty percent up front will grease the skids."

Cathy looked at her sister, who nodded in agreement to move on this. Cathy took her checkbook out of her leather bag and wrote a forty-five-hundred-dollar check to Agent Brambly's business—*Surveillance Is Our Business, Inc.*

"You will not regret your decision to go with us. You will not know that we are there—go about your business as usual. I'll get in touch with you; don't try to reach me. Believe me, Mrs. Dimmer, I'll catch him if he is cheating. They never only cheat once," he told Cathy as he took the check from her extended hand.

This comment only added to Cathy's discomfort.

"So you are on duty now?"

"Yes, like gum on a shoe."

"Good," Cathy said, meeting Agent Brambly's eyes. They rose from the table, shook hands, and left the shabby office strewn with file folders—with her file folder now on top of the heap.

As they walked to the car, Carole, holding Cathy's arm, spoke softly. "You've done the right thing. You've protected your wealth in a trust and will soon know if Jake is cheating."

In her heart Cathy knew that her sister was right, but she still felt a nagging sadness all over. She needed to act as though nothing had changed. The truth was everything had changed.

****

"Barry Silversmith phoned. He wants you to call him back pronto," the receptionist told Burt Brambly.

"Will do," Brambly answered, and he dialed Barry's number. The firm had him on retainer, paid well, and kept *S.O.B.* very busy.

"Burt Brambly returning Attorney Silversmith's call," he told the receptionist at the law offices.

"I'll put you right through," Burt heard the receptionist say.

"Thanks for returning my call. I need you to help me clear my client by getting me all the information you can on the comings and goings of a Jake Dimmer. Can you do that for me ASAP?" Barry asked his friend.

"Funny that you should ask that question. I've just been engaged by Jake Dimmer's wife to do the same thing. Is your client a woman?" Burt asked in confidence.

"No, my client is not a woman. As far as I can tell, Jake is framing my client for murder and ..."

"What?" Brambly interrupted.

"You know that I can't tell you anything else. Just get me whatever you can on Jake Dimmer," Barry said and ended the call.

Chapter 9

BUD WAS WAITING FOR ROSA's arrival from Boston on the afternoon fast ferry to Provincetown. He sat on a bench under the pavilion at the end of MacMillan Pier, where he had a good view of the harbor. In the old times, he and Rosa traveled together to solve some big cases. They were compatible. They knew each other very well. He never regretted joining RAID when she asked him to. He appreciated that Rosa let him take FBI special cases. More than anything, today he was grateful that she was coming to lend whatever help she could on the lighthouse murder case—even though she was supposed to be on a Cape Cod vacation.

Bud was shaken from his thoughts when he spotted the fast ferry moving past the bell buoy and heading toward MacMillan Pier to dock.

As soon as the fast ferry was secured to the dock, the passengers began to disembark onto the pier. Hundreds of vacationers and day visitors from Boston, dragging or carrying luggage, poured out from the ferry to the pier boardwalk. Among the smiling visitors, happy to be on vacation, came a tall, brown-eyed woman with shiny mahogany hair in a ponytail, wearing a navy baseball cap, a flowered blouse, navy chinos, and sandals. She carried a camera bag over her shoulder and pulled her suitcase behind her. She scanned the waiting crowd, and her gaze stopped on the handsome, blue-eyed Bud, who was looking in her direction. Her smile widened, and she headed to where Bud was waiting.

He came toward her and wrapped his arms around her. Bud whispered, "I'm so glad that you're here."

Rosa hugged him back but drew back just a bit to feign looking at him, and Bud reluctantly let her go. Stepping back from Bud she said, "Any place for an ice cream cone?"

"You bet," he answered and took her suitcase as they headed arm in arm to town along the pier boardwalk.

"As you were saying at our dinner in the city with Guy, the case you're working on is a puzzle."

"It is. I would appreciate your take on what I have so far," he answered as they arrived at the corner ice cream shop.

Rosa ordered a small Moose Tracks cone. Bud ordered a large Chocolate Peanut-Butter Cup waffle cone. Out on the street the two sauntered along eating ice cream in a stream of tourists. They wandered west on Commercial Street to the benches in front of the town hall. They took their seats with the tourists to sit in the sun and eat and people watch.

Rosa was taken by the scenery. "I love what I am seeing on Commercial Street: the old wooden retail stores and restaurants, the tourists on skateboards, bicycles making their way through streams of tourists walking in the street and on the sidewalk, families walking on the sidewalks and in the street with baby carriages. I'm especially taken by the street musicians, the face painters, and the balloon man making balloon animals for the kids." Just as Rosa took some more ice cream, a drag queen in a clown costume rode by on his bicycle calling to come to his afternoon show. She laughed.

"I didn't know what to expect when the FBI assigned me here with this case. It has a charm of its own. People seem to accept each other as they are," Bud said.

Bud suggested they get the car and head to the condo so that Rosa could get refreshed. Pulling Rosa's suitcase behind him, Bud and Rosa walked to the parking lot to retrieve the car.

A short time later at the condo, Rosa took in the evening harbor view from the deck. With a glass of wine and music in the background, she looked over the bobbing boats and slowly moving sailboats. "*Wow!*" was all she said as they sat on comfy chairs on the deck watching the sunset paint the sky.

"Rosa, I thought I had the case all figured out, and then the suspect threw an unexpected curveball into the story. He fingered his identical twin brother for the crime. He denied being in Provincetown with his brother on the day of the crime. He tried to frame his brother into a lifestyle he didn't agree with. I am more convinced than ever that we have the right suspect. I need to figure out how to prove it," he told Rosa.

"From what I remember you saying at dinner in New York, it may have been a crime of passion, an accidental death."

"Yes. It is complicated because the suspect is married to a New York debutante, and the victim was a young man here in Provincetown."

"I see. What leads you to suspect that you have it right and that the suspect's twin is innocent?" Rosa asked, trying to make sense of what might have happened on that day on the beach.

"We have traced the license plate number of the car seen at the apartment and picking up the victim at work to a Jake Dimmer, our suspect. But we have items in the victim's apartment that point to the twin. We are waiting for DNA information of skin under the victim's fingernails. We already have semen samples from the victim's body indicating two different men, the victim and someone else."

"Then why are we in Provincetown? You need DNA samples from your suspect and his twin, don't you?" Rosa probed.

"I need more information about the victim that I want to double-check from the victim's employer here in town. I need to talk with the whale-watch captain to see if he puts the twin on the boat during the time of the crime. And, yes, I need to get DNA from my suspect and his twin brother; for that I will go to Boston."

"Good. Let's get started. What do you know about the victim now?" Rosa asked.

"He was a young man, about twenty-three, living in Provincetown. He worked as a waiter at a year-round restaurant. He loved to party. His employer told Detective Santos that he met the suspect a year or so ago. The neighbors said that Arthur told them that sometimes they would stay out all night, often on the beach after the bars closed. Frequently, when they came home at dawn, his friend would leave immediately in his SUV.

"Have you talked to his employer yet?" Rosa questioned.

"Not yet. Detective Santos, here in the Provincetown Police Department, is working the local piece of the case. She mentioned the frequent pickup of the victim at his workplace. You'll meet her tomorrow," he told Rosa.

"Okay." Rosa watched the sunset firing across the sky in reds and yellows. She turned, glass in hand, to see Bud lighting up the grill.

"Tonight is grilled yellow-fin tuna with a green salad," he announced.

Rosa thoroughly enjoyed being wined and dined in the company of her dearest friend. The smell of fresh salt air, aroma of grilling fish, and the taste of delicious wine was a rare moment to savor.

Over dinner on the deck, Bud and Rosa continued to talk shop. Before Bud left New York, he had arranged for two undercover FBI agents to trail Mr. and Mrs. Dimmer, twenty-four seven.

"Good idea. What are your plans for our search here tomorrow?" Rosa asked, tasting her tuna and sipping her wine.

"I want to check with Detective Santos on where she is on the case. Then I'll know what I'll need to do," Bud answered, lifting his wineglass to toast.

He felt content that Rosa was on board even if only for a short time.

Chapter 10

ROSA WAS ALREADY SITTING ON the deck, coffee in hand, taking in the magnificent views, when she heard Bud arrive from the kitchen with a plate of newly made blueberry scones in one hand and a pot of freshly brewed coffee in the other.

"I'm so glad that I decided to come to visit Provincetown. It has to be one of the most beautiful places on earth, with blue skies and twinkling water," Rosa told him while reaching for a warm scone.

"After we talk with Detective Santos this morning, would you like a tour?" Bud asked Rosa.

"That sounds good, being that this is my first visit to the town at the end of the world!"

It was shortly before eight when they left the condo for the Provincetown police station. Detective Santos was preparing for her morning shift as Bud and Rosa appeared at her office door.

"Good morning. The dispatcher told us where to find you," Bud said to a startled detective, who was deep in thought.

"Hi, Bud. Great to have you back," she said, looking first at Bud and then at Rosa. "Who is this?"

"I want you to meet Rosa Arroya. She is here visiting for a few days," he told Santos.

"Nice to meet you. Are you the Rosa Arroya who heads up RAID?" she asked.

"Yes. Bud and I go back a long way. It's nice to be here," Rosa said tactfully.

The detective nodded at Rosa and said to Bud, "Let me give you a rundown on what we know," motioning to her computer desk.

"Grab a couple chairs," she told them. "Let me begin with the coroner's report," she said, pulling up the report on her computer screen. "The death was by suffocation due to strangulation by a belt around the neck. The coroner's report explains that this sort of thing can happen in sex games. He proposes that the death occurred because neither the victim nor whoever was with him could or chose not to release the belt before he lost consciousness and his life. According to the forensic evidence, someone else was with him," the detective added.

"How do they know someone else was present?" Bud wanted to know.

"The forensic report says here that semen from two people was found on Milne, who had recently ejaculated. The question is was it murder?"

"Do you mean that the other person may not have been able to free the belt in time? On the other hand, maybe he panicked about the situation and deliberately did not loosen the belt in time," Bud speculated. "Sounds like I need to find the belt."

"The lab is testing for DNA of the semen and of skin taken from under the victim's fingernails. Once we have that information, we'll check our DNA database for a match for the second person," Detective Santos told them.

"Did you check in with the victim's employer?" Bud asked.

"Yes. We verified his identification with the restaurant owner," Santos responded.

"I want to do some follow-up with the employer," Bud told her.

"Go for it. Can't hurt."

Rosa and Bud thanked the detective for her time and update on the case, got up, and made their way out of the police station.

At the car, Bud said, "I need to do more footwork on the comings and goings of the suspect, especially his contact with Milne. I think that his employer may be able to shed some light on that."

"Sounds like a good place to begin our day. Have you considered a whale watch today?" Rosa said, reminding Bud that she was still on vacation.

"Why don't we do the whale watch first? We need to park the car at MacMillan Pier parking lot anyway."

"Sounds right to me," Rosa said, thrilled to be going on her first whale watch.

"Gus Gilmore, captain of the *Dauphin XXI*, has been highly recommended by Detective Santos. He runs the premier whale watch and education trip," Bud mentioned.

As they arrived at the *Dauphin XXI*, Captain Gus Gilmore was waiting to welcome the passengers. "Welcome aboard. Hope you are ready for a great whale watching trip today."

Soon after the boat got underway and headed out of the Provincetown harbor, the captain announced over the loudspeaker, "A quick word on safety: Do not stand up on the benches. Watch the children and do not let them run on the vessel. We are sure to see some minke and finback whales and maybe a North Atlantic right whale. Enjoy the trip."

Bud and Rosa waited until the announcements were finished and then approached the helm to talk with the captain. The room was neatly organized, with a depth finder and compass in front of the captain's chair. There was a cabinet just inside on the right of the door to the room.

"Captain Gilmore, I'm Detective Bud Black, and this is Detective Rosa Arroya," Bud told him as he showed his credentials.

"Nice to meet you," the weathered-faced captain answered, keeping his eyes on the expansive bay ahead.

"Captain, we have an impossible task. We need to establish the whereabouts of this man in Provincetown a week ago," Bud said to the captain and showed him a photo of Jimmy Dimmer.

The captain looked carefully at the photo of Dr. Jimmy Dimmer. "If he was on my whale watch vessel, we'll have his picture boarding the boat. We do souvenir photos for the summer tourists," the captain told them.

"This may be our lucky day. Can we see the photos?" Rosa asked, peering around the organized room.

"You'll find a metal box in the cabinet over there by the wall. The photo duplicates are in there. Good luck!" the captain said.

Bud and Rosa sat at a small table in the cabin to get started on their search. The captain announced over the loudspeaker to look to the right side of the vessel at several finback whales. The vessel immediately lurched to the right as the passengers rushed to see the whales and to take pictures. Rosa couldn't resist a look and left her seat to stand next to the captain, who gave her his binoculars. "Cool!" uttered Rosa.

There were thousands of photos dated and time-stamped. Near the middle of the heap of pictures, Rosa came across a photo that matched Bud's picture of Jimmy Dimmer. The photo was dated mid morning the day of the murder. Jimmy was in Provincetown on a whale watch as he had said. At least Jimmy would have been returning from the whale watch in the afternoon. The question was, did he leave Provincetown or did he stay? Rosa gave the picture to Bud after the captain gave an okay nod. "Glad we could help," he said.

"Bud, we need to establish that Jake Dimmer was also in Provincetown that day. According to the record, Jimmy said that his brother usually dropped him off at the pier and went off on business," Rosa said, beginning to put some of the puzzle together in her mind.

"When we get back to town, I want to talk with Milne's employer at the restaurant," Bud said, as he too began to put the pieces of the case together.

They thanked the captain profusely and replaced the pictures in the metal box. They saved the one of Jimmy Dimmer, put the box away in the cabinet, and left the room to enjoy the rest of the whale watch.

****

As all the passengers disembarked from the *Dauphin XXI*, Bud and Rosa headed for the beachfront eatery on Commercial Street where Arthur Milne had been a waiter. The Seafood Shack was packed with noontime guests.

The host, a young man with an Eastern European accent, welcomed them with a smile and asked, "Two for lunch?"

"Yes," Bud and Rosa answered in unison.

The young man led them to a window seat overlooking the beach and placed two menus on the table for them.

"Sir, we are here to talk with the owner. Is he here?" Rosa asked.

"I'll get him for you," the host responded and moved toward the kitchen.

A waitress arrived at their table and asked if they wanted a drink to start the meal.

"We're on vacation—why not?" Rosa said to Bud.

After some discussion, they both ordered white peach mojitos and a shared order of fried clams.

Moments later, the owner, a small, round, balding man approached them. "You wanted to see me?" he said to them.

"Yes. I'm Detective Black and this is Detective Arroya," Bud answered and stood to shake the owner's hand. "We'd like to ask you a few questions about a previous employee, Mr. Milne," Bud continued. He sat again, and the owner pulled up a chair to join them.

"Oh, that poor boy. I feel so badly about his death. He was a gregarious and reliable employee," the owner said in a low voice.

Bud pulled a photo he had of Jake Dimmer and the photo they had just found on the *Dauphin XXI* of his twin, Jim Dimmer, from his pocket and asked, "Do you recognize either of these men?"

"They both look like Arthur's friend. He came here usually on weekends in a silver Cadillac SUV to pick Arthur up after his day shift."

"How often did he do that?" Rosa asked.

"I'd say every weekend, and sometimes in the middle of the week, over the last year and a half—well, until recently, that is," he responded.

"Thank you, sir. You've been very helpful," Rosa said as their drinks arrived with a huge order of fried clams.

"I want to be helpful in any way that I can," the owner said as he left them to enjoy their drinks and food.

"Hmm. This case just got more complicated with Milne's employer identifying the photos as the same person. Why are the twins both lying? Jake says he wasn't here, and Jimmy says he hasn't seen his brother often since they were kids, but did agree that they were here last weekend."

"Milne's employer and the whale watch captain, Gilmore, have put some very important pieces of this puzzle into place," Rosa added, sipping her mojito. "By the way, when do you expect to hear from the undercover agents you have watching Jake?" she added.

"They text me updates daily," Bud answered, somewhat distracted by his own thoughts about the day's findings. "You know, Jimmy Dimmer may have only hitched a few rides with his brother. He may not have known how often Jake actually came here."

Rosa shook her head in agreement. "True. We only found one whale watch photo of Jimmy, but Milne's friend had the Cadillac," she added.

They finished up their drinks and fried clams, and paid and tipped the waitress before they left the Seafood Shack to wander through Commercial Street on their way to the parking lot to get Bud's car. On the way, Bud received a texted message from the agents tracking Jake. He read it and raised his eyes to meet Rosa's.

"News?" she asked.

"Yes. Cathy, Jake, and the two FBI agents are ready to board a flight to the Cayman Islands!" he answered.

"Did you know of this trip?" Rosa wanted to know.

"Yes. I was aware. When I talked with Cathy Dimmer, Jake's wife, she mentioned it, but seemed less than enthusiastic about going on what she called a last-minute vacation," Bud explained.

"Anything else?" Rosa asked.

"The text also says that there seems to be someone else following the couple," Bud added.

"That's interesting. Who could that be?" Rosa asked.

"If I let my mind wander, I can think of a few scenarios. Jake may have his own plans for Cathy, based on Cathy's hesitation about this trip. She seemed concerned about the suddenness of the 'getaway.' I'm beginning to think that Jake would do anything to protect his current lifestyle, and a fear that Cathy would find out could put him over the edge."

"On the other hand, maybe Cathy hired a private investigator for her own protection and wants to find out who this man, Jake, is that she married," added Rosa.

"Either way, the case just became even more complicated," Bud confessed.

Before they got to the pier parking lot, Bud caught sight of the trolley tour parked in front of town hall.

It was a beautiful day in Provincetown, and Rosa was happy to be enjoying it with Bud. She was pleased to help Bud's case however she could. Most of all, she was glad to have Bud as her tour guide as they hopped onto the trolley tour.

Chapter 11

THE FLIGHT FROM JFK INTERNATIONAL Airport in New York to the Cayman Islands left on time with Jake and Cathy Dimmer on board. In the rear of the plane sat the undercover agents. Other than a crying child reacting to the altitude changes on takeoff and landing, the flight was uneventful.

Jake was sweet and attentive with Cathy, who had reluctantly agreed to come on the last-minute getaway.

Cathy tried to be herself when responding to Jake's new burst of attentiveness. She had been a theater and drama major in college. She was very convincing.

The two undercover agents assigned by Bud, and Mr. Brambly, the detective hired by Cathy and Jimmy Dimmer's lawyer, had scattered themselves throughout the cabin of the plane, all within visible distance of the "loving couple." Bud's agents were aware of Mr. Brambly, and Mr. Brambly was focused on the Dimmers.

While Bud's agents were talking about the upcoming destination, Brambly was feigning reading a book.

"What do you know about the Cayman Islands?" Agent Stewart asked Agent Curley.

"Not much," replied Curley.

"I've heard that there are more registered businesses than residents," Stewart added.

"Ha! Really? Must be a good place to launder money," Curley contributed.

"A friend of mine came here with his family to snorkel. They stayed on Seven Mile Beach near the capital, George Town," Stewart shared.

"From what he told me, they had a great time in the clear waters and totally loved the food."

"I've heard that scuba diving is big here too," Curley added to their information on the Cayman Islands.

"I've been to a lot of places, but this will be my first visit to the Cayman Islands," Stewart admitted.

"Mine too. Not quite sure what to expect," Curley confessed.

"Oh, I got the travel agent Jake used to plan this trip to give me more details of the island," Stewart told Curley.

"Like what details?" asked Curley.

"Like the hotel name, Barrier Beach Resort, for this three-day getaway special that includes dinner with champagne, and a scuba trip," he answered.

"Are we on the same plan?" Curley asked.

"Yes. We are traveling as a couple!" Stewart laughed.

"*What?*" Curley leaned forward, astonished by this new information.

"Calm down. Bud is convinced that our boy is a switch-hitter, and we might have some luck proving it," Stewart responded.

"What do you have in mind?" Curley asked, trying to stay calm.

"We'll take photos in any compromising situation we may find him in," answered Stewart, having thought about this for a while.

"This scheme seems a bit of a stretch when the guy is traveling with his wife, don't you think? I'd be more concerned about the scuba trip he has planned," Curley told Stewart.

The loudspeakers blared, "*We are beginning our descent and arrival into the Cayman Islands. Be sure that your seat is in the upright position and that your seat belt is fastened.*"

After the hectic disembarking from the plane, the passengers filed off on their way to collect their luggage and go through customs. Outside the terminal, people scattered to get taxis, rent cars, and meet folks picking them up. Agents Stewart and Curley hung back to watch for the Dimmers and their tail. A tour agent for this getaway held a sign with names—Mr. and Mrs. Dimmer, Mr. Stewart, and Mr. Curley. The four assembled near the tour agent, who ushered them to a small van that would take them to the hotel for their getaway visit. Undercover agent Brambly hailed a taxi and followed the van.

The van ride to the resort was quiet. Not even "Hello, my name is ..." or "*Wow*, this is beautiful!" Not a word from anyone until they got out of the van and said thank you to the driver who was helping with the luggage and receiving tips.

The resort, Barrier Beach Resort, was set up for the diving set, with scuba tanks and equipment prominently placed near the entrance where they came into the lobby. The Dimmers were first to check in. The agents, Stewart and Curly, came to the reception desk next. They had overheard the room number of the Dimmers, and with a glance at each other, acknowledged the information. Curley noticed both Cathy and Jake glancing in their direction. He smirked to himself and lifted his shoulders, feeling his ego and thinking *this may be fun after all*.

They also noticed that Cathy was very upset by the confirmation of a scuba trip. "We discussed this at home. You know I get claustrophobic!" she said to Jake through clenched teeth at the desk.

After check-in and on their way to the room, Curley told Stewart, "I'm sure Jake was giving me the eye."

"Did you give him 'the eye' back?" Stewart asked, smiling from the corner of his mouth.

"Shut up!" he answered.

"Perfect. Now he is really interested," Stewart responded. "By the way, I saw the hefty, round guy who is following the Dimmers come into the lobby as we were leaving the reception desk."

"Boy, this is a crowded three-day holiday. Should we check him out?" Curley asked Stewart.

"Yes. In due time," Stewart answered as they arrived at their water-view room on the beach level just steps away from the pool.

Sitting on the patio, Curley and Stewart perused the situation. Soon the hefty, round man found his way to a poolside lounge chair across from the Dimmers, who were now seated at the pool end nearest the beach and ocean. It seemed like Cathy was arguing with Jake over something—probably the scuba trip scheduled for the next morning. The agents decided to get closer to the action and walked over to the poolside lounge chairs nearest the Dimmers. Stewart began fawning over Curley, showing him caring attention as they set up their chairs with towels. Both agents extended a friendly hello to the Dimmers. Jake smiled and nodded hello back to them, while noticeably looking at both men with interest. Cathy was all smiles and seemingly very happy that the men had decided to sit nearby. Actually, she had her eyes on Stewart and seemed oblivious to the "couple" thing.

Soon everyone had drinks and had dipped into the pool. In the water, Cathy swam laps while Jake stood near a waterfall. The agents hung out closer to Jake. Brambly stayed on his lounge chair drinking his fruit drink and watching. Stewart left Jake and Curley to swim laps. Curley was left alone to fend for himself with Jake.

"Do you come here often?" Jake asked Curley, now just feet away.

Curley tossed his hair and smiled. "No. This is *our* first trip here," he answered, trying to play the role as best he could.

"I come here quite often, but it's my wife's first trip here," Jake told him.

"We have a special getaway that includes a scuba trip tomorrow morning," Curley told Jake.

"Us too, but my wife is less than enthusiastic," Jake admitted.

"Well, she sure is a good swimmer." Curley nodded toward Cathy, who cut through the water with the ease of a seasoned swimmer.

Curley saw Stewart talking with Cathy at the other end of the pool. Jake had moved even closer to him and was giving him a flirtatious look. Raising his arms over his head, Curley dove into the pool and swam away from the waterfall and Jake.

Stewart and Cathy had returned in what looked like a swim race. Laughing, they lifted themselves out of the pool and fell into their lounge chairs and towels by the pool. Curley reached their side of the pool and hopped out to get his towel and join Stewart. Jake sloshed slowly back, stood waist-deep in the pool, and let his eyes take in the entire collection of people before him. It was just about time to freshen up for champagne and dinner. The Dimmers were the first to leave the pool area to get ready for dinner.

"He's a letch!" hissed Curley to Stewart.

"What happened?"

"He would have fooled around in the pool had I given him the slightest encouragement," Curley explained. "He flirted with me."

"Okay. We might have something starting here to prove Bud's theory. Let's see what happens later," Stewart told Curley.

"What do you mean, later?"

"Don't worry. I'll be near to take a picture and to intercede, should I have to," Stewart told him.

Curley did not like the situation he had been thrown into. On the other hand, if this letch was after him and cheating on his beautiful wife, he needed to be caught. *What a rat*, he thought and although it wasn't illegal, it would surely help the murder investigation.

"Did you get to talk with Cathy?" Curley asked.

"Not much. She is definitely distracted on this trip. I'm not sure what's going on," Stewart answered.

They gathered their towels and went back to their room to get ready for dinner in the simple, colorful dining room.

In the dining room, two tables marked *Reserved* were set with champagne bottles in ice buckets. The Dimmers were already seated at one of the tables, drinking their champagne. The two agents went to the other table. A waiter opened the champagne, served it to each of them, provided two menus, and left.

In the shadows of the dining room sat a big man alone at a table for two, his eyes on the Dimmers.

The evening became a tricky set of "who is following whom?" After dinner, agents Stewart and Curley walked on the beach a short distance behind the Dimmers, while Investigator Brambly followed them. The moonlight showed the way along the beach by the water's edge.

There was a lot of animated conversation between Jake and Cathy, using arm gestures and a sudden shove almost causing Cathy to fall. It did not seem like playful fooling around. It seemed more like an argument with heated tempers, or at least a serious disagreement becoming physical. Stewart and Curley had managed to slip into the shadows, and pulling out a pair of night goggles from Stewart's backpack, Curley focused on the couple.

"You know, I think the guy following the Dimmers is a detective," Curley told Stewart as they watched the big man taking pictures with his night camera of the couple fighting.

"Well, Bud didn't give him the assignment. Did Jake?" Stewart whispered.

"Or was it Cathy?" Curley added, taking a close-up picture of the big man.

As they were watching, they saw Cathy slap Jake. He struck her back. Soon fists were swinging, voices shouting, and entangled bodies wrestling down to the beach. Curley, Stewart, and Brambly raced to the scene to stop the fight. Brambly reached the couple first and grabbed Jake off Cathy and threw him to the sand. Cathy ran to Stewart for protection, and Jake, stumbling as fast as he could, rose to his feet and lunged at Brambly. Brambly met Jake with an armlock around his neck. Cathy shouted *"Stop!"* to everyone. Jake fell to his knees in the sand and cried out, "I'm sorry. I'm sorry." Cathy left Stewart's protecting arms and approached her sobbing husband on the beach. Brambly decided to leave quietly, seeing that the two men the couple had befriended seemed to be there to keep the peace. Curley helped Cathy get Jake to his feet. The four walked back single file along the water's edge to the resort. Jake kept saying, "I'm sorry. I'm sorry."

Agent Stewart sat on the hotel bed and texted a message to Bud, informing him of the situation. He said, *"All things percolating. Third agent on Dimmers' tail? Tonight we broke up domestic fight between Cathy and Jake on beach. He was drinking too much. Jake has his eye on Curley! Tomorrow big day—scuba trip."*

Chapter 12

BUD AND ROSA SAT DOWN with Detective Santos at the Provincetown Police station to go over their combined findings on the case. Bud brought forward that Jimmy Dimmer was indeed in Provincetown on the weekend in question, but had a firm alibi that he was on a whale watch and not in the vicinity of Court Street or the Long Point lighthouse. Rosa added that Jake Dimmer, on the other hand, was in Provincetown every weekend for the past year and a half, according to Arthur Milne's employer, having picked Arthur up every Friday after his shift at the restaurant. Detective Santos had the best news of all. They now had the medical examiner's report, toxicology/drug screen, and DNA results from the victim's body.

"Looks like drugs and alcohol played a big part in this tragedy. The evidence we have points to a sex game gone very wrong. Two sets of male DNA, one from the victim, have been identified from the semen on the victim's body. The belt marks around his neck are consistent with strangulation and the cause of his death. It would be good if we could find the belt," she told Bud and Rosa as they all pored over the report.

"We have a problem. The brothers are identical twins. Jake has denied being here on that weekend, even though Jimmy said he hitched a ride with Jake to get here," said Bud.

"Neither of them knows of the mounting evidence we have gathered putting them both in Provincetown," Rosa shared.

"True. Jake has already implicated his twin by telling us that Jimmy frequented Provincetown, and has an alibi claiming a business trip to Philadelphia," Bud shared.

"Two things: discredit the Philadelphia alibi, and confront Jake with the evidence putting him in Provincetown," offered Detective Santos.

"At the moment, Jake and his wife, Cathy, are in the Cayman Islands, and Jimmy is watching their dog," Bud told the detective.

"What?"

"I have them under surveillance, and expect them to return to New York in a couple of days," Bud told Santos.

"Meantime, let's put more pressure on Jimmy," suggested Rosa, feeling the need to get Jimmy on board in the investigation.

Rosa and Bud thanked Detective Santos for her update, and left for a final few hours of vacation. They would leave for New York City later and another visit with Guy Fox at the NYPD.

Bud and Rosa got into his car outside of the police station and headed to Herring Cove Beach for a lunch stop. Before they could park, Bud received a text message from his agents in the Cayman Islands.

"Today could be challenging—scuba trip," was all it said.

Bud turned to Rosa. "Things could be heating up with Jake and Cathy," he told her.

"Considering the scuffle you told me about on the beach last night and Cathy's reluctance to go on this trip in the first place, I think you're right. Even my adventurous spirit would take pause regarding a scuba trip in those circumstances," Rosa added.

Leaving the car, they both wandered over to the concession stand. The ocean roared below them as they sipped their soda and ate sandwiches from the concession stand.

Later at the rented condo, they packed their things and loaded their suitcases into the car to return to New York City. Rosa had an idea.

"We need to confront Jimmy with the evidence before we confront Jake," she said.

"Why do you say that?" Bud asked.

"He has to know that this is serious and that Jake is setting him up for the fall. He needs to roll on his brother."

"And just how do you propose to do that, considering his reluctance so far?" Bud asked as they got into the car.

"Jimmy doesn't know me. I'll go, wear a wire, and get him to talk candidly with me," she offered.

"No doubt in my mind that you know how to do this, considering your fame in bringing the perps in," Bud told her.

Rosa smiled. She had a plan.

Chapter 13

THE WATERS OF THE CARIBBEAN were warm and a bit choppy as the four people on the special getaway scuba trip boarded the boat. A guide was talking with the guests about the equipment, its use, and safety measures.

"Who here has been scuba diving?" the guide asked.

All but Cathy raised their hands.

"Good, that makes life a bit easier," said the guide, handing the necessary flippers and scuba gear to each person to put on as the boat found its way to the reef that they would explore.

Agents Stewart and Curley put their suits and equipment on, while Jake made sure to help Cathy get ready. The guide came to each person to check his or her equipment and to give the okay for the dive. A second guide back-flipped from the boat into the clear, warm, blue water and waited for the group to do the same, one at a time. Agent Stewart put his back to the water, held his mask in place, and flipped backward, tank first, into the water. Agent Curley followed. Jake encouraged Cathy to take the plunge next. She was reluctant. She pointed to him to go first, but he was shaking his head no.

Finally the guide returned to the boat to find out what was wrong. Cathy was crying and grasping at the mask; her claustrophobia had taken over. Jake was insisting that she'd be okay and told the guide to go ahead, that he'd be responsible for Cathy. The guide refused to leave Cathy in such distress and ordered Jake to remove her mask. By this time agents Stewart and Curley were back on board in time to hear the argument between the guide and Jake over the removal of Cathy's mask. Cathy was gasping for air, and the guide stepped between Jake and Cathy and removed her mask. He noticed that the air hose was pinched closed and asked, "How did this happen?" No one answered.

Cathy was beginning to feel ill. The guides considered ending the dive to head back to shore, apologizing profusely to the two men for the situation and promising a refund or credit, whichever they wanted. Stewart and Curley agreed to end the trip, noticing that Cathy wasn't well. Once again, the four were silent, as another incident between Jake and Cathy changed a day of adventure into a day of suspicion. Did Jake pinch the hose on Cathy's equipment? Neither Stewart nor Curley could say for sure, but circumstances pointed in that direction.

When the boat got back to shore and they all felt the sand on their feet, Stewart suggested that they all go for a drink. But the atmosphere did not lend itself to a friendly drink among newfound acquaintances. Cathy thanked Stewart for trying to help lighten a trying situation, but declined. Jake followed her off the beach toward their room at the resort under the watchful eye of Brambly, who was relieved that they had all returned as he sat by the poolside reading and sunning himself.

"What will he try next?" Curley asked Stewart as they each settled by the pool with a Mai tai for each of them.

"I'm not sure, but he has his hands full with all the watchful eyes on him," Agent Stewart said, watching the big man watching Cathy and Jake as they headed toward their room, both less than happily. Jake was trying to be attentive, but Cathy was irritated. Stewart decided to text Bud.

"Seems like JD has plans to harm CD. Close call on scuba trip. Day not over yet."

It was time to bug Jake's room. The agents concocted a scheme to get Cathy and Jake to come to the lobby reception to clear up some confusion stemming from the scuba trip and a refund. Curley was especially good at opening locked doors. During that time, they planted the bug in Cathy and Jake's room, entering from the interior hallway.

"But, sir, there must be a misunderstanding. The two men on the trip with us are due a refund, not us," said Jake, with Cathy by his side at the reception desk.

"No. The two men on the trip with you insisted on giving you their credit for another trip sometime," the receptionist told them. "As a matter of fact, we wish to give you a personal refund, Mrs. Dimmer."

"You can give them their refund or credit; we will not be using it or mine," Cathy said. *"Ever!"*

"Oh. I'm sorry. Was there a problem?" the receptionist asked.

"No. Now please remove the credit from our bill and give it to the men who were on the trip with us," Jake said roughly, waiting to see that the receptionist did as he commanded.

There had been plenty of time for the agents to plant the bug. In fact, the suspicious Brambly had arrived to see what they were doing in the Dimmers' room. Everyone had met now, with introductions all around, handshakes, and assurances that they were all on the same page in this particular surveillance job. Cathy was in danger. Brambly explained that Cathy was sure that her husband had a mistress and wanted proof. She thought that she might be in danger if Jake wanted her out of the way so that he could be with his lover, while getting the inheritance from his very wealthy wife. The agents told Brambly that their suspicions were that Cathy was in danger for a different reason. They told him that they believed that Jake was a switch-hitter, afraid of the truth, and Cathy's ire if she found out. They moved quickly from the room to the pool area again, the two agents separating from Brambly, as they had been before they had formally met. They all sat down around the pool to watch the bathers and the balcony of the couple's room.

"I can't believe that the men would give us their trip credit considering how much I did not like the idea in the first place," Cathy said to Jake as they entered the elevator going to their third-floor room.

"Maybe, like me, they thought that you would come around to the idea at another time," Jake told her, trying to implant a message of both guilt and encouragement.

"You know full well that I'm claustrophobic," she said, her voice rising. "How would I ever like my eyes and nose closed into a scuba mask with an oxygen mouthpiece for air?" Her frustration had reached a peak, and when the elevator stopped at the third floor and the door opened, she shouted, "You said that I could go along for the ride. You never said that you expected me to scuba dive."

She was at a breaking point. Jake drew back from Cathy; it had only been a day and a half of the three-day getaway. He wanted to get drunk. He wanted to get her drunk. He was desperate to figure this out. Surely he could make her death look like an accident.

"Why don't you go get yourself some dinner and a few drinks?" Cathy told him as she pushed past him to get to the room. "I'm in need of some quiet time alone."

"Are you sure?' he asked, feeling relieved that he didn't have to make the same suggestion for himself.

"Believe me, I'm sure," she said curtly.

Jake went to the bathroom, where he showered and put on aftershave, his Caribbean shorts, and white cotton see-through shirt, which he left mostly unbuttoned against his tanned chest. He slipped into his new Italian leather sandals. On the way out, he tapped on the closed bedroom door to say good-bye, but there was no response.

In the lobby Jake stopped at the desk to ask for information about clubs on the island.

Agent Curley saw Cathy sitting on the balcony porch alone. From where he sat, he could see the lobby, where Jake was talking with the receptionist.

"I think our boy is on the move," Curley told Stewart.

"Then I guess that you better be on the move too. I'll keep my eye on Cathy," Stewart told him.

"Brambly is doing that. You need to come with me," Curley told him. He appreciated Agent Stewart's feelings for the endangered Cathy, but he needed Stewart to be with him.

The two agents, in shorts and loose-fitting colorful cotton shirts, headed to the lobby in time to hear the remnants of a conversation about island clubs for single men. They were careful to stay their distance, out of sight, as Jake headed to the door to get a taxi.

"Where did you recommend he go?" Stewart asked the receptionist, who was still fingering the phone book he had used. He wrote down the name of the club and handed it to Stewart.

The agents watched the taxi at the door pull away with Jake in it. They got the next one.

"Follow that taxi ahead of us," Curley told the driver. "We're going to the same place," he added.

The two taxis moved into the heart of the town and then off to a desolated area just outside of the town center. The first taxi stopped at a club hidden in the tropical vegetation to let Jake out. He didn't bother to look around and proceeded into the club's dark entrance, surrounded by low lights and a hint of disco music.

"I don't like the looks of this. Looks too rundown and isolated for me," whispered Stewart as the two exited the taxi.

They entered the club. It was dark, a bit musty, with thumping disco music. Tanned-bodied men in shorts and muscle shirts were dancing together to the rhythm under dim lighting. Other men were sitting at the bar eying anyone who entered the place. Other male couples were making out in dark private booths. Drinks were flowing freely from the looks of things. Stewart noticed the sweet smell of pot smoke.

Jake had managed to find a vacant bar stool and took a moment to look around. Agents Curley and Stewart found a dark booth, slid in out of view, and kept their eyes on Jake.

It didn't take long before Jake was dancing seductively with a young, handsome man under the dim lighting on the dance floor. Curley secretly took a picture, the first of many compromising shots of Jake at the club that night. At some point in the evening, Jake and a poster boy-type young man disappeared into a back room for more privacy. The agents had gotten what they came for and phoned for the taxi to come get them.

Stewart texted Bud. *"JD definitely switch-hitter!"*

Chapter 14

T HE BACKGROUND INFORMATION ON JIM Dimmer in the FBI file indicated that he liked jazz, played a guitar, and was attentive to his mother. Rosa's plan to trail Jimmy to a jazz club for the Tuesday-night jam session he often attended worked like a charm. She disguised herself as a coed at NYU majoring in science. She wore a blonde, short, sporty wig, dark-rimmed glasses, jeans, and an Eric Clapton T-shirt. Jimmy noticed her immediately. He liked what he saw.

Rosa was seated alone at a small table centered in front of the jazz ensemble getting ready to start jamming. She was sipping a vodka tonic with lime. She had a biology text with her to work on while the music played. Considering that Jim Dimmer was a dental surgeon, Rosa believed that a biology text would complete the coed student impression she wanted to make on him. Meanwhile, Jimmy was sitting at the bar observing the patrons through a large bar mirror.

After the first jam session, Jimmy approached Rosa. "Hi," he said. "I haven't seen you here before. Are you enjoying the jazz?" he asked.

"Oh, yes. I love jazz," she answered. "I'm usually studying with my study group on Tuesday nights. Tonight, I needed a break. I've wanted to come to this club all semester. So far tonight, I'm glad that I did," she said flirtatiously, smiling at him.

"Would you mind if I joined you?" he asked her. "My name is Jim Dimmer."

"Sure. There's room for two," she answered, realizing how easy this was going to be.

"What's your name?" he asked innocently.

"Maria," she answered.

They sat listening to the jam session until the break, then continued talking with each other. He asked about the biology course she was taking at NYU, and fingered through the text she had on the table. He told her he was a dentist and had loved his biology courses almost as much as he loved jazz. She probed carefully into his life, as she was so good at doing in cases like this. He was quick to tell her that he was a twin. He seemed very relaxed with Rosa and found it easy to emote on his lonely life. Rosa was taken by his gentle, honest nature. She liked him immediately. She became more determined than ever to help clear his name from this tragic crime.

As the evening went on, Rosa was astonished at how much she knew about Jim Dimmer's life. He knew precious little about hers, and what he knew was a lie. The first time Rosa had seen Jim was in the interrogation room at the NYPD when Bud questioned him. She looked nothing like an NYU coed, and clearly Jim did not recognize her tonight. The evening ended and the club cleared out.

"Can I walk you to your dorm?" he asked Rosa. "It's late and you shouldn't walk alone," he added.

"I'm taking the subway to my brother's place tonight," she told him, and they walked toward the subway entrance.

"Oh. Will I be able to see you again?" he asked, hoping he was not coming on too strong, in that they had had such a nice evening of conversation and good music.

"Yes. I'd like that. I've found you very interesting," she told him.

He smiled. It wasn't often that Jim Dimmer met someone like this. They seemed to share a lot of common interests—music, travel, and the seashore. He handed her a business card with his office phone number and address on it. "Please call me when you get back to the city. Maybe we could have lunch together," he suggested.

"I'll do that," she told him, smiled, and went down the steps to the subway below.

She entered the waiting subway train, went one stop, and came up to the street to hail a taxi. She and Bud were staying at a small hotel near the NYPD headquarters. They had an appointment with Captain Guy Fox in the morning. Rosa would share the news of her progress on Jimmy Dimmer and her renewed belief that he was totally innocent.

When Rosa got to her hotel room, she saw a flashing light on the room phone. It was very late, and she wondered if she should check it out or wait until morning. Reluctantly she pressed the message button and listened to the caller. "Call me whenever you get in!" She recognized Bud's voice. He seemed concerned.

Rosa called immediately and awakened Bud out of a sound sleep. "Hello," he slurred.

"Bud, is Rosa. You wanted me to phone. What's up?" she asked him.

He shook his head, rubbed his eyes, sat up in the bed, and answered, "I have confirmation that JD is a switch-hitter."

"Good. I think this could have waited until the morning, don't you? I'm exhausted. Talk to you later. Good night," she said and hung up. She knew that the news was major and that Bud knew he was on the right track in this case.

"Good night," he said to the empty line. And dropping the receiver onto its base, he was fast asleep again.

Chapter 15

THE GETAWAY TO THE CAYMAN Islands had put some pieces of the case into place. The two agents had evidence of Jake's proclivity toward men, and suspicion of his desire to get rid of his wife. Brambly was convinced that Cathy was in danger, as she had suspected, but had no evidence of Jake's wandering eye for other women. The flight didn't leave until six that night, so there was a full day for Jake to cause harm to Cathy. Both agents and Investigator Brambly were on high alert.

Agents Stewart and Curley perched themselves by the pool in view of the Dimmers' balcony. Investigator Brambly sat at a small table at the pool bar in position to watch the beach and the lobby. It was early, and the guests were busy getting their lounge chairs, towels, and mimosas in preparation for the day to come. Stewart, Curley, and Brambly didn't know what to expect, but they expected something was going to happen between Jake and Cathy before the van came for their departure to the airport that afternoon at four.

"You don't think that Jake would take Cathy to swim with the stingrays, do you?" Curley asked Stewart.

"That is one more adventure they haven't had yet," Stewart answered. "I don't think so. It is too open. As far I can see, Cathy is a much better swimmer than Jake. She could turn the tables on him in a water environment."

As the two contemplated what Jake had in mind for the day, they saw Cathy on the balcony. She was crying. Then they heard her shout, "I really don't care what you do today. I'm staying here by the pool."

They heard a door slam. Cathy remained on the balcony a few minutes more before coming to the poolside alone.

Brambly spotted Jake in the lobby and decided to follow him. Again, Jake took a taxi and Brambly took another taxi. "Follow that cab," Brambly instructed as the taxi moved away carrying Jake.

Cathy approached Stewart and Curley. "Would you mind if I sat here with you today?"

"Not at all. Can I get you a drink?" Stewart gushed over her. Curley rolled his eyes at the overt display of affection Stewart showed Cathy.

The three sat, read, and swam off and on, and finally decided to go to the bar for lunch together. It was over lunch that Cathy began to talk.

"I don't know where Jake found this three-day getaway. It was supposed to help our relationship, but it has made matters worse," she confessed to the two men.

Curley looked at Stewart with a gesture that meant, "Let's tell her who we are."

"Cathy," Stewart began, "we are FBI agents hired to track Jake."

Cathy was shocked at first. "FBI? Oh my." Cathy was noticeably relieved. "Oh, thank heavens," she blurted out, tears welling up and spilling down her cheeks. "I've been in fear for my life during this whole trip," she moaned.

"What can you tell us about Jake's travels?" Curley asked gently.

"Today he is off on some business meeting. He plans to be back by three this afternoon," she answered.

"Is it common for him to have business meetings?" Curley asked, trying not to seem to pry too much.

"During the past year or so, he has been away more than he has been home. It is always a business trip. He assures me that it is a lucrative venture for our future," Cathy shared.

"How much did you know about Jake before you married, if you don't mind me asking?" Stewart queried.

"I must admit that he took my breath away with his charisma, good looks, and what I thought was wealth," she answered.

"What do you mean what you 'thought was wealth'?" Curley asked.

"I'm not sure where he gets his money. He says that he is self-employed in his own company. He spends money freely on big-ticket items like his condo on the Hudson, a place for his mother, a flashy car, and trips all over the place. And now this unplanned getaway."

"Is he violent toward you?" Agent Stewart asked.

"No. He is very gentle, although controlling. But lately, he has been different. I can't explain it. Something has changed him. I think that he has a mistress," she explained.

The agents listened, looked at each other, and shared a look that said, "Say nothing."

Cathy continued her story. "I have been so upset that before I came on this trip, I saw my family lawyer, and hired a detective to find out just who Jake's mistress is."

"That was a good idea," encouraged Agent Stewart, with Agent Curley nodding his head in agreement.

It was midafternoon when the three decided to pack their things for the four o'clock van ride to the airport. Their all-inclusive getaway was about to end.

In the meantime, Brambly found himself at a seedy club playing pool alone and watching Jake pick up a young man at the bar. He was able to get a few good shots of Jake and his new friend dancing. Jake and the young man had begun the late morning with drinks and seductive dancing, and eventually they disappeared behind a curtain for more privacy. Brambly couldn't see if drugs were also involved, but he knew now that Jake probably did not have a mistress. He had boyfriends!

At four o'clock sharp, and after Jake's return to the hotel, the van arrived at the resort to take the four getaway guests to the airport for their evening flight back to New York's John F. Kennedy International Airport. First at the door were the two agents, followed moments later by Cathy and Jake. There were cordial acknowledgements all around as they watched the driver place the luggage into the van. They all got into the van for a silent ride to the airport. Agent Curley spotted Brambly heading for the next taxi waiting at the door of the resort.

The six o'clock flight left on time, with Cathy and Jake sitting in view of Stewart, Curley, and Brambly. During a bathroom break by Agent Stewart, Brambly made his way to the restroom in time to make contact with Stewart in the aisle.

"Just wanted to tell you that I have photos of Jake's morning business meeting," Brambly told Stewart as he flashed him the photos on his iPhone.

"Excellent," Stewart whispered. "I wonder if you would e-mail them to me?"

"Let me be sure that my client agrees first. This is going to be a big blow to her. I need to be sensitive about it," Brambly told Stewart.

"I understand. Remember, our case is about murder, and you have a piece of very important evidence," Agent Stewart reminded him.

"I won't hinder your investigation. I just want some time to tell Mrs. Dimmer first," Brambly insisted.

Brambly and Stewart returned to their seats in time to prepare for landing. They were all satisfied that the getaway had been worthwhile. Agent Curley had sent Bud an update on their findings. He had asked if they should stay on the case now that things were beginning to fall into place.

The question of Cathy's safety remained on each agent's mind.

Chapter 16

Jake barely talked to Cathy all the way home from the Cayman Islands. In their New York penthouse apartment, Cathy asked point-blank, "Do you love me?"

The question caught Jake totally off guard. "Of course I love you," he stammered but made no attempt to approach Cathy and turned his head away from her.

"I have felt you becoming distant from me over the last year or so. Do you have a mistress?" She finally asked the question that had been burning in her heart all these months.

Jake couldn't help himself and began to laugh. It was a strange laugh of relief and joy that Cathy was unaware of his secret. He did not want to lose her in divorce. He wanted things to stay the same. He composed himself and looked into her eyes and lied. "There is no one in the world that I would rather spend my life with than you, Mrs. Cathy Astor Dimmer."

This time Cathy saw through the charade, and laughed at him even louder than he had laughed at her comment. "Jake, are you expecting me to believe a lie?" she asked, feeling stronger than ever, knowing that she had secured her wealth into a trust and that soon she would have a report from Brambly on his mistress.

Jake was totally surprised by this sudden change in Cathy. She had never challenged him or not believed whatever he told her. He felt a surge of anger at her defiance. He grabbed her by the shoulders and shook her. When she pushed him away, he hugged her and pleaded for forgiveness. "I'm sorry. You know that I would never hurt you. I love you," he repeated, releasing her from his embrace. She rubbed her arms where he had held her and shaken her.

"You hurt me, you fool," she said, pushing him away. She shouted at him while continuing to rub her arms and fighting back tears. "I don't even know who you are anymore, Jake. What is going on?" she asked, looking him straight in the eyes. She wanted some answers. She was on the verge of divorcing him, but she wanted the truth of what had happened between them.

"Honest, baby, nothing is wrong. I may be a bit stressed by work, that's all," he lied again.

"Work? What do you sell? Who are your clients? I know nothing of what you are up to on all these business trips lately. Even the FBI asked me about your work and I was clueless," she pressed.

"The FBI? Did they talk to you again?" He was noticeably shaken by that reality.

"I know that you are involved in something, Jake. The FBI would not be asking questions about your business schedule of trips otherwise. They suspect you of something. Do you want to tell me, or would you rather they tell me?" she asked him.

Jake began to sweat. This was the question he couldn't—and wouldn't—answer. He needed Cathy to focus on Jim, not on him. He couldn't face the truth, the truth he had hidden for almost two years. The truth that would end his marriage, he believed. No, he would deny, deny, deny. He would convince her to believe him. "I'm just working too hard," he insisted. "You know that I'm doing it for us, for our future security."

"I don't believe you. I feel like you have become a stranger to me. Jake, I am asking you to be honest with me. Tell me the truth. If you love me so, surely you can trust me with the truth," she pleaded.

Jake needed a drink—something to calm him. His hands had begun to shake. He realized that he was coming down from the doxepin antidepressant he had taken this morning to steel him for the evening flight and conflict he feared was to come. Maybe he should take another pill.

"Give me some time. Let me show you that everything is okay. I need some air," he said and headed toward the penthouse elevator to leave. He was sweating heavily now. He knew where he could go to feel better.

"That's right, Jake, run away. Go wherever you go when you leave me here for hours on end. Run away from yourself; see if you can." She was shouting. "You're doing a good job running from me!" she yelled as she walked into the bedroom and slammed the door.

Jake felt that things were not going well for him. It was time to bring Jimmy into his plan to make him look guilty. He would lure Jimmy to their mother's place to implement his plan.

Jake went into the elevator, down to the lobby, and out to the dark street. Outside he felt the cold night air on his moist face. He hailed a taxi and got in. "Take me to the village," he told the driver.

But Jake was not alone. Brambly was on his tail.

Chapter 17

Rosa and Bud met for breakfast at the corner donut shop before their meeting with Guy Fox at NYPD headquarters. Both had lots to tell the other from their findings the night before.

"Sorry I awakened you last night," Rosa began.

"Oh, that was okay. I guess I expected you to come home a bit earlier," he chided her.

"You sound like my father," she retorted.

"Sorry. I guess I did, didn't I?" he agreed.

"I'm making inroads with Jim Dimmer. He wants to see me again, for lunch," Rosa told Bud, now wide-awake and listening to every word she had to say.

"How long will it take to put some closure on this with him, do you think?" Bud questioned.

"He is very vulnerable and seems to be a bit of a loner. I need to be careful not to toy with him only to let him feel betrayed," Rosa explained.

"What does that mean? Are you pulling the plug on this part of our plan?" Bud asked with great concern.

"I'm not sure. I like this guy, and I really don't want to hurt him," she told Bud.

"Then, what about telling him the truth the next time you see him?" Bud asked.

"I've thought about that. I don't want him to clam up or get defensive either," she answered.

"Rosa, you have done this so many times. You're one of the best agents in the world at disguise and capture. What makes this time any different?" Bud was curious.

"He is a twin. The bond between identical twins is fierce. I'm not sure that I can be successful this time," she admitted reluctantly.

"Think of it this way. Jim Dimmer is going down for a murder he did not commit. Is that what you want?" Bud reminded her.

"You're right. I can't leave him hanging out to dry like that. He needs my help, even if he doesn't know it yet," she agreed with renewed commitment.

"Good. That sounds more like the Rosa that I have known. And we now know that Jake likes men!" he told her with a sound of satisfaction.

"Yes, that information is critical to my work with Jim," she agreed as they finished their coffee and donuts, and continued to NYPD headquarters.

Guy Fox was waiting in his office when Rosa and Bud arrived for their morning meeting.

"Coffee anyone?" Guy asked as they entered his office.

"No takers. We just finished ours," Bud told him, with Rosa by the desk nodding in agreement.

"What do you have on the case so far?" Guy asked them.

Bud began. "I know these five things: Jim Dimmer has been framed for the murder, Jake is our number-one suspect, we have just validated that Jake likes men, we suspect that Cathy Dimmer is in danger for her life, and Rosa is working with Jim to get him to roll over on his brother."

"Why would Jim roll over on his brother?" asked Guy, looking at Rosa.

"It is very complicated in that Jim and Jake are identical twins. Jake has dumped on Jim since they were kids and gotten away with it, according to Jim's own words. Jim doesn't realize that the evidence we believe was planted by his brother is very damning. I have to convince Jim that he is in real trouble and that Jake has made it so," she answered.

"What can Jim say to help himself out of the mess?" Guy continued.

"He needs to be honest with us about the days in question. We know that both Jake and Jim were in Provincetown on the weekend of the murder. We have proof that Jim was on a whale watch most of the day. We know that Jake picked up his boyfriend at his workplace the evening of the murder. We can place Jake and the victim together on numerous weekends in Provincetown. We have DNA from the victim and another male. We need to get a DNA sample from the twins, unless we can find a match in the DNA data files currently being searched. The FBI suspects that Jake is a drug lord. They have been watching his travels back and forth from Mexico and the Caymans, according to their records. Their theory would explain his unaccounted-for wealth. We need Jim to admit that Jake drove him to Provincetown that weekend. We think that Jake was not in Philadelphia on business, as he says he was. We're checking the contact Jake has in Philadelphia. We think the alibi is very flimsy," Bud told Guy.

"What can I do to help?" Guy asked.

"Let me work with Jim a bit more before we make a move to arrest him. He only has an alibi during the day of the whale watch. What did he do that evening?" Rosa added.

"I want to lay a trap for Jake. I want him to believe that he is in the clear," Bud added.

"How do you propose to snag him?" Guy asked.

"I'm still working on that, but I'll need your help when the time comes."

"You can count on it," he told Bud. "It is time for this guy to be brought to justice."

Rosa and Bud both thanked Guy for his assistance and willingness to get involved with the FBI, and headed out of his office and back to their hotel to plan the day.

Rosa contacted Jim Dimmer for another meeting, and Bud touched base with Agents Stewart and Curley for a debriefing on the Cayman Islands trip. Bud was pleased with the agents' findings and observations of Jake in the Caymans. Bud had evidence of Jake's proclivity for men, a major piece in the case. Still, Bud felt uncomfortable that Cathy might be in danger.

Chapter 18

ROSA PUT ON HER DISGUISE as Maria for her second meeting with Jim Dimmer. They would meet for lunch at one of New York's four-star Indian restaurants in the East Village. She called Jim to confirm the restaurant's address before she left the hotel.

"Hello," he answered. "Something has come up, Maria. I can't meet you for lunch today," Jim Dimmer told Rosa. "I wanted to call you, but didn't have your number."

"Your voice sounds stressed; is something wrong?" she asked him.

"I can't talk just now. Call me tomorrow," he said and hung up.

Jake had called Jimmy and told him to meet at his mother's place in Tarrytown, New York, because the cops were closing in on Jimmy.

Jimmy dropped everything, rearranged his appointments, and went to his mother's place as fast as he could on the afternoon train.

Jake was already there when Jimmy arrived. Jake met him at the door with a big hug and hard slap on Jimmy's back. "Glad you decided to come so quickly, Jimmy," Jake told him.

Jimmy went to his mother and gave her a hug and kiss on her cheek.

"What's all the fuss about, boys?" she asked.

"Nothing, Ma, everything is under control; just a big misunderstanding, that's all," Jake told her.

"Yeah, Mom, everything will work itself out," Jimmy added.

"Jimmy has to take a trip to Montreal on today's bus out of town," Jake continued.

"Is that the best thing to do?" Jimmy asked his brother.

"Yes. They won't expect you to go to Canada. Hey, let me make us all a cup of tea before you go, what do you say?" Jake piped up.

"I have some fresh cookies, your favorites, in the cookie box in the kitchen," Mrs. Jasper told Jake.

"Sure, I would like that," Jimmy answered.

Jake took the opportunity to carry out his latest plan to get Jimmy to run, making him look guilty. Jake had brought doxepin with him and planned to lace Jimmy's tea with enough to drug him. As Jimmy helped his mother lay out the cookies, Jake prepared the tea. Before bringing the cups of tea to the table, he glanced over his shoulder and then placed two doxepin tablets in one of the steaming cups of tea. Feeling quite smug, he stirred the tea until the doxepin disappeared. The plan was set. If Jimmy survived the drug, it would at least look like guilt drove him to a suicide or an attempted suicide. Jake had no sense of guilt over this idea—none! Not as long as it cast more suspicion onto Jimmy.

He served the tea and cookies to his mother and Jimmy. Jake was quick to tell Jimmy, "The bus leaves in thirty minutes; you don't want to miss it!"

Jimmy agreed and hurried his tea and cookies, hugged his mother, and said good-bye.

He took a taxi to the bus station from his mother's. He felt conflicted about the rush to leave, but trusted his brother to make the right decisions.

Jimmy got his ticket at the ticket counter at the bus station and boarded the bus. He was beginning to feel a bit light-headed.

****

In New York City Rosa put the receiver down onto the phone and thought a moment before she phoned Bud on his cell phone.

"What's up?" she heard Bud ask when he answered his phone.

"Something is wrong. Jim hastily canceled our lunch plans; he sounded stressed and said that he couldn't talk about it now," Rosa told Bud.

"Let's pay the doctor a visit at his office," Bud suggested. "I'm a few minutes away from the hotel; I'll pick you up," he told her.

Rosa stayed in her coed disguise and went to the lobby to watch for Bud's car. A few moments later, she was in Bud's car and they were on their way to Jim Dimmer's dental office.

As they pulled up in front of the office, they saw a sign placed in the window of the front door:

"Closed today—sorry for the inconvenience."

Rosa and Bud parked their car and approached the closed door. Bud knocked hard. "FBI, *anyone here?*" Bud called. They waited, listened for sounds inside, and hearing nothing, entered the office lobby. There was a quiet eeriness about the room. Everything was in its place, nothing was disturbed, and no one was around. They walked beyond the lobby to the dental rooms, consultation offices, and finally to Dr. Dimmer's office. Only the scattered papers on his desk betrayed him—he would have been under duress to leave his desk in such disarray.

Rosa spoke first. "Do you think that Jim was spooked by his brother into running?"

"I am thinking the same thing. His brother could have made it eminently clear to Jim that he was going to be arrested for murder," Bud offered.

"Of course, running screams 'guilty,'" Rosa said.

"We need to find Jim. He is making a big mistake, because he has us on his side; he shouldn't run," Bud said while wondering where to begin.

"I have a cell phone number. I'll try that," Rosa said, pulling her phone from her pocket and tapping in the number for Jimmy Dimmer.

A few rings and then a few more rings were unanswered. She tried again. No answer.

"We need a trace on his phone," Rosa advised, and they left the dental office as they had found it and headed to the NYPD headquarters for assistance.

"Do you think that Jim would go to his mother's before disappearing?" Rosa asked on a hunch.

"Definitely a possibility, considering their closeness and his frequent visits to see her," Bud agreed.

"Let's pay her a visit or at least telephone her today," Rosa suggested.

"We'll have the information we need at the NYPD. Shouldn't be very difficult to find."

Minutes later, at the NYPD in Guy's office, Rosa was on the telephone talking with Jim's remarried mother. "Mrs. Jasper, my name is Rosa Arroya. I'm a private investigator working with the FBI. Can I ask you a few questions, please?"

"What is this about?" Mrs. Jasper snapped.

"We want to talk with Jim. Is he there?" Rosa asked.

"He was here. The boys were here. Jim is taking a trip and came to say good-bye. Why?"

"How long ago was that?" Rosa pursued.

"About ten minutes ago. He was in a rush to get the bus. Why do you want to talk to Jim?"

"The bus to where? Did he say?" Rosa continued.

"Not really. Something about Montreal."

"Thank you so much, Mrs. Jasper. Good-bye." Rosa ended the call and turned to Bud and Guy.

"If the information Mrs. Jasper gave me is accurate, Jim Dimmer is on his way to Montreal by bus, today," Rosa shared with them.

"I want every bus from Tarrytown, New York, to Montreal stopped and searched for Dr. Dimmer, *now*," Bud yelled in frustration to Guy. "Guy, this is one of those times I mentioned when we need your help."

"You've got it." Guy picked up the phone and ordered the dragnet. "We'll find him. I'm sending his photo out with the call to search every bus on its way to Montreal," Guy assured them.   Popping his head back into the office doorway, Guy addressed Rosa. "I take it you are in disguise for your role in this case?"

"Why, yes. Do you like my preppy look?" she teased back.

"I love her preppy look," chimed in Bud. The mood had become a bit lighter. "It reminds me of when we first met years ago."

"You guys are just jealous that you are not a 'preppy' like I am!" she retorted playfully. They all laughed. Their light moment was quickly changed when the phone rang in Guy's office.

"Captain Fox here." He listened. "Uh-hmm.... Yes, bring him in. We'll meet you at the hospital."

"What happened?" Bud and Rosa asked in unison.

"Not sure. They found him unconscious on the bus at the Canadian border. The ambulance is bringing him back to Einstein for observation and tests. We'll meet them there."

Bud was more concerned than ever. He feared that the family dynamics were about to get very ugly.

Chapter 19

A T THE HOSPITAL, ROSA AND Bud, with an NYPD police officer, reviewed the medical report on Jim Dimmer. He had been drugged, but it was unclear what the substance had been or where he had gotten it. He was in and out of a deep sleep. During one of his conscious moments, Rosa, on a hunch, asked Jim two questions.

"Jim," she said softly, "can you remember if Jake was at your mother's house when you visited earlier today?"

Weak and drowsy, Jim nodded his head yes.

"Was it your brother who encouraged you to travel to Canada?" she continued gently.

Again he nodded yes, and closed his eyes to sleep.

A doctor entered the room. Picking up Jim's chart, he told Rosa, "You'll have to leave now. He is too weak to respond to any more questions."

"Thank you, doctor. Will he be okay?" Rosa inquired.

"We are giving him activated charcoal. He's had a gastric lavage; we pumped his stomach, and he is as you can see on intravenous fluids. We'll keep our eyes on him during the next twenty-four hours. We don't know if damage has been done to his liver. Our toxicology screening indicates an overdose of doxepin, a tricyclic antidepressant. The other test results will be ready soon. He has no record of taking this drug on his medical record. Now, I have to attend to him. Excuse us," said the doctor, who went to Jim's left side and drew the privacy curtain around the bed.

The NYPD officer was posted outside the room for security purposes. Jim was wanted for additional questioning, and Bud had asked Guy for the extra NYPD protection. Rosa and Bud left the hospital, fully convinced that Jake was involved in the overdose as well as scaring his brother into running. Jim was in great danger because he was still alive, thanks to quick-acting EMTs at the bus stop, where a traveler alerted the bus driver that a man was unconscious and was having trouble breathing. The police arrived at the scene and realized that the patient was wanted by the NYPD. The EMTs' fast reactions saved Jim's life.

There remained questions on how the drug was obtained. Was there a prescription for it, and who had the prescription? Who was the doctor who prescribed the medication? There was no record of Jim taking the antidepressant in his medical history chart. His access to the drug was in question. The hospital doctors continued testing Jim for other blood indicators that could explain the condition he was in.

Rosa and Bud were quick to track down Jake Dimmer's doctor. They headed to his office to get some answers regarding Jake's medications.

"Can I help you?" asked a pleasant receptionist at the doctor's office as Rosa and Bud entered the area and closed the door behind.

"We are FBI agents," Bud said, flashing his badge. "We are here to talk with the doctor."

A stunned receptionist quickly buzzed the doctor. "There are two FBI agents here to see you."

The doctor appeared at his door and invited them into his office. "You are here at a good time; I'm in between patients," he cheerfully told them.

"Nice to meet you. I'm FBI Agent Bud Black, and this is Agent Rosa Arroya," Bud said while extending his hand to the doctor.

"Please take a seat. What can I do for you?" he asked after shaking their hands.

"We want to know if Jake Dimmer is a patient of yours."

"Yes, he is," the doctor answered. "Why do you ask?"

"Can you tell us if you have prescribed an antidepressant for him?" Bud asked.

"Now I know that you both know full well that that is privileged information."

"We do. But in this case, the drug has been abused, and in fact could have been used to attempt to kill someone. This information is part of a murder investigation. We can get a warrant for the release of

Jake's medical record, or you can answer our question and save everyone a lot of trouble," Bud explained.

"I feel very uncomfortable releasing that information," the doctor responded.

Rosa spoke up. "Just nod your head yes or no to my question," she told him. "Do you think that it is highly likely that Jake has a prescription for doxepin?"

The doctor reluctantly nodded his head yes.

"Thank you for your help," Bud told him as Rosa and he stood up to leave the office.

On their way to the car, Rosa said, "We need to visit Jake before he tries to finish the job on Jimmy."

"I agree. Evidence is mounting on Jake, and he may be feeling the pressure," Bud told Rosa as they headed uptown to Jake Dimmer's residence.

They talked about how to set the trap, how to unnerve Jake, how to tell him just enough to push him into making a mistake. They would have him where they wanted him.

Chapter 20

INVESTIGATOR BRAMBLY WAS NOT LOOKING forward to his meeting with Cathy Dimmer this morning. He sat fidgeting at his desk with various reports, photographs, and expense vouchers. In his mind he was trying to work out the best way to report his findings to Cathy. It wasn't going to be easy.

It was ten o'clock when Cathy and Carole arrived for her discussion with Brambly. She thought that she was prepared for the news.

"Hello, Mrs. Dimmer, Carole" the big man said as he came from behind his desk, smiled, and offered two chairs.

"Good morning," she answered, and they sat down on the chairs he offered in front of his desk to hear the report.

"Mrs. Dimmer, I really don't know exactly where to begin."

"Just tell me the truth. How old is she? Where does she live? Is she beautiful?" Cathy asked.

Brambly swallowed hard, cleared his throat, and began, "Mrs. Dimmer, please look at these photographs from the Cayman Islands trip, and a few I took last night at a men's bar in the village."

He spread out a dozen photos for Cathy to see—some distance and some close-up. All the pictures had Jake front and center, with handsome, young men dancing closely, embracing, and kissing. There could be no question that Jake was enjoying himself.

Cathy was speechless as she looked at the pictures over and over again. "No, this can't be true," she said again and again as she continued to shuffle through the photographs. "I can't believe this. Why? Is he gay?" Carole was notably surprised at the report.

"Forgive me, Mrs. Dimmer, but Jake seems to enjoy the company of men," Brambly said, trying to buffer the harsh reality of the photographs.

"I really *do not* understand," Cathy shouted, slamming the photos down on the desk.

"I'm so sorry. This is a tough way to find out about something like this."

"Maybe this was the first time. Maybe he was angry at me. Maybe it is my fault that he was driven to do such a thing." Carole put an understanding arm around her distressed sister.

"If you want my opinion, Mrs. Dimmer, Jake has been involved in this behavior for at least as long as you have been suspicious of a mistress in his life."

Cathy burst into tears. Her husband had broken all the trust she had had for him. The worst was that he had broken it for a man, not another woman. Brambly offered her some tissues.

Brambly gathered together the written report on the investigation, copies of the photographs, and his final bill and handed them to Cathy. "Mrs. Dimmer, the FBI asked me for the photographs. Will you release them to the FBI through me?"

Cathy, having almost gotten herself together, was again taken by surprise.

"Surely they can get their own photographs," she snapped.

"Yes, they have their own photos. They know that I have these and can demand that I turn them over. I'd rather be cooperative if I can," he told Cathy.

"I don't seem to have a choice, do I?" she said with irritation.

"Not really. I wanted you to know and to agree before I complied with the request," he answered.

"I appreciate your thoughtfulness, Mr. Brambly. It's okay. Who cares?" Cathy said in resignation as she took a checkbook out from her purse and wrote a check for the balance due Brambly.

"Mrs. Dimmer, if I can be of any other assistance to you, please don't hesitate to engage me," he told her and took the check she offered to him.

"You have been very professional, and I like your forthrightness. You can call me Cathy," she told him with a stressed smile as she gathered his report and photos into her purse to leave. She was noticeably shaken by the news, but showed great emotional restraint in front of Investigator Brambly after the initial shock.

Brambly watched Cathy and Carole leave his office. He had mixed emotions of satisfaction in completing the investigation, and sadness for Cathy and the turmoil ahead of her in this rocky relationship. In a way, he'd love to see her again. Maybe one day under different circumstances, he would.

Chapter 21

J AKE WAS PACING AROUND THE penthouse wondering where Cathy was at this dinner hour. She was always here preparing his meal, handing him a cocktail, giving him a welcome-home kiss. She had not mentioned any reason that she would not be home tonight—or had he forgotten?

Their relationship had been cooling for a while, but it was especially noticeable since the first FBI visit, followed by the stressful trip to the Cayman Islands, as well as his own preoccupation with his secret life. His mind began to race with paranoia. *What if she suspects something? What if she knows about my Provincetown trips? What if the FBI has spoken to her again? "Snap out of it!"* he told himself and shook his head as though to clear away a fog.

Through the noise in his mind, he heard someone buzzing to enter the penthouse elevator.

"Who is it?" he called through the speaker.

"FBI Agents Bud Black and Rosa Arroya."

"Just a minute," he called, having an instant reaction with shivers, profuse sweating, and nausea. He went to the liquor cabinet, pulled the bourbon bottle from the shelf, and poured himself a glass of bourbon over ice. He took several big gulps, took a deep breath, and buzzed the agents into the elevator to come up to the penthouse.

Jake met the agents at the elevator door. "Good evening. Can I be of some help to you?" he asked, role-playing calm.

"Good evening, Jake. Are you alone, or is Mrs. Dimmer at home too?" Bud asked.

"I've just come home, and I expect Cathy to arrive any minute," he answered.

"We have some unsettling information on the murder case in Provincetown," Rosa told Jake.

"Oh?" Jake felt a sharp stab go down his left arm, and he gulped the last of the bourbon and rattled the ice in the glass.

"Maybe we should wait for your wife to come home, so that you both hear the information at the same time," Bud offered, watching Jake's demeanor and discomfort grow.

"No. Let's proceed. I can tell her whatever she needs to know," Jake answered.

"Jake, new evidence completely exonerates your brother, Jimmy, from any suspicion in the Provincetown murder."

"Wow! That's great news," Jake said, pouring another drink of bourbon over the remaining ice in his glass. He felt a wave of sweat overcome him.

"It is very good news for Jim, but not such good news for you!" Rosa added, watching Jake steady himself against a chair.

"What do you mean, not good news for me?"

At that moment, Cathy entered the penthouse from the elevator. The conversation stopped, and everyone tuned toward her.

"Hi, honey." Jake moved to hug her, but was rebuffed. "We have company," he added, looking back at the two agents.

Cathy walked toward Bud and Rosa. "Hello," she said with a flat tone and sat down on the leather recliner next to where Rosa stood. "Please, don't let me interfere with the conversation," she told them.

"Do we have to do this now?" asked Jake, now nervously holding a glass of melting ice.

"I think that what we have to say is very important for you both to hear," Bud responded.

"Yes, I'd love to hear what you have to say," Cathy chimed in, clearly armed for whatever the agents had to say after her visit with Investigator Brambly.

"Maybe we should all sit down," Rosa suggested.

With empty glass in hand, Jake sat on the largest leather chair. Bud and Rosa took to the couch, and Cathy remained in the recliner.

"The evidence completely exonerates Jimmy Dimmer from any suspicion in the Provincetown murder," Bud stated for Cathy to hear.

"We were just saying that this is great news for Jake's brother. The problem is that it is not good news for Jake."

"What does that mean, not good news for Jake? He'd do anything to help his brother," Cathy said, eying Jake nervously tapping his foot.

"It means that Jake is under suspicion for murder, Mrs. Dimmer," Bud responded, looking straight at Jake Dimmer.

"That is absurd!" slurred Jake.

"I hope that you have proof before you make such an accusation," Cathy said. Cathy looked startled and searched the faces of her husband and the FBI agents.

"Mrs. Dimmer, we do not take lightly the evidence in a murder case. I can assure you the evidence is mounting against your husband," Rosa told Cathy.

"I think that you both need to leave our home now." Jake struggled to be clear in his directive, speaking slowly and pointing toward the elevator door.

Bud and Rosa rose from the couch, said good night, warned Jake not to travel from New York, and left by the elevator as they had arrived.

Cathy got up from the recliner and walked to Jake, now slumped over in his chair. She stood looking at him in his pitiful state. "You are a total stranger to me. I have no idea who you are or why we ever married. I want a divorce!"

"Divorce? Divorce? No one is getting a divorce," he shouted as he struggled his way out of the chair and stumbled across the room to the arm of the couch to steady himself. He remained standing, holding onto the back of the couch.

"I don't want to be married to you anymore. I don't even love you," Cathy yelled back at him as she headed toward the bedroom.

"Where do you think you're going?" he yelled and lunged at her as she tried to pass him steadying himself by the couch. He grabbed hold of her shoulder. She twisted away and pushed him against the back of the couch. They struggled until both lost their balance and fell to the floor. Cathy struggled against his drunken strength to free herself. She kicked at him with a free foot, only to feel his arms tighten around her chest and his head press hard into her back. She could barely breathe as he held her ever tighter. She gathered all her strength, raised her arm over her head, and reached for his full head of curly hair pressed between her shoulders. She grabbed a handful of hair and pulled with all her might. It was enough to break his viselike grip around her. She turned toward him, his body on hers, and with the strength she had left, plunged her knee into his groin. She heard him moan, felt him double over, totally freeing his grip on her, and roll off. She crawled away as fast as she could, stood, and ran to the bedroom, closing and locking the door behind her. She heard him pounding at the door and yelling. Fearing for her life, she dialed 911.

"Open the door, bitch. Open the door!"

The 911 operator asked Cathy for her address. "He's trying to break down the door. He's drunk—hurry," Cathy yelled into the receiver, and she sputtered her address, dropped the receiver, and rushed to the bureau to push it against the door. She stood back, shaking. She held her arms tightly around herself and stared at the door.

"Open this goddamn door before I tear it off its hinges!" his angry voice demanded.

"No, Jake. You're drunk; go away!" Cathy yelled back.

Several thuds came against the door as Jake beat at it. He exploded in angry words as he continued to crash against the door. Suddenly there was silence. Cathy wasn't sure what to do. Then she heard Jake's voice: "No, officer, no one called for help from this apartment."

Cathy rushed to the phone and dialed 911 again. When the operator answered, Cathy said, "This is Cathy Dimmer again. There is an officer here right now, but I have barricaded myself in the bedroom, and my husband is denying that anyone called for help. He is sending him away. I need help! Please, please tell the officer to stay," Cathy pleaded with the 911 operator.

"I need your address, madam," the operator told Cathy.

"I just called you a few minutes ago; surely you have my address. I need help now!"

"Try to stay calm. Help is on the way," Cathy heard the operator tell her.

Cathy went to the bedroom door and listened. She heard Jake and the officer talking.

"You need to leave," Jake was saying to the officer, who was taking a call on his cell phone.

"I see. Yes," the officer said into the phone. He put it away and walked toward Jake.

"I have asked you to leave; now I'm telling you to leave," Jake said sternly.

"I have been told that this is the apartment that called for help—not once but twice," the officer told Jake in no uncertain terms. He called out, "Cathy Dimmer, are you here? This is the police."

Cathy heard the policeman and quickly shoved the bureau away from the door. She flung open the bedroom door and ran to the living room, where both men stood.

"Please take him out of here, officer. He's drunk and is being abusive to me. I want to press charges," she told the policeman.

"She is having one of her paranoid fits. Don't believe her story. I don't know what she is talking about," Jake insisted.

"You wretched man," Cathy yelled. She pleaded with the policeman, "Please arrest him. I don't feel safe here with him," she told the officer.

At that moment a female officer arrived at the penthouse elevator door and entered the apartment. "What's the problem?" she asked.

"There is no problem," Jake yelled at her.

"We have a she said-he said situation, and he smells of alcohol," answered the first officer.

"He tried to kill me. He physically tackled me and tried to crush my chest. I could barely breathe. I was able to get away and barricade myself in the bedroom. I called 911 for help. I only came out when the officer arrived and called for me. Before you came, he was pounding on the bedroom door, yelling and threatening me," Cathy told the officers in desperation.

"She's lying. She tackled me and kicked me," Jake told the officers to counter the accusation and sounded perfectly sober.

"He's lying. You can't believe him. I'm in danger," Cathy said, still shaking.

"Everybody needs a cooling-off period. The best thing to do is for both of you to come with us to the precinct. Cathy, if you still want to press charges, you can do it there," the first officer told them.

"Oh, that's just crazy. So now we go to the precinct, you talk to us separately, and we cool down, when there was no problem to begin with, unless you believe this sick woman's story," Jake told the officers.

"Our dispatcher believed this woman's story—that's why I'm here," said the second officer. "Cathy, come with me," she continued, reaching her hand out to Cathy's arm and leading her out of the apartment and down the elevator to one of two patrol cars outside.

Jake went with the other officer to his patrol car, resigned that he had no choice, but he was ready to cement the idea that Cathy was sick in her mind with jealousy, delusions, and paranoia.

****

At the precinct the Dimmers were taken separately and questioned about the incident. Jake spun a tale of Cathy's mental health issues and delusions about a fight that was nothing but a marital tussle.

Cathy told the truth about the confrontation following her demand for a divorce. She wanted to press charges of physical abuse. She had some bruises on her arms. The police were finding themselves in a difficult situation. Both stories were plausible. Cathy began to sense that her story was being torpedoed by Jake's story, with whatever lies he was telling.

"I want to call Mr. Brambly, a private investigator I hired. He can verify my fear of Jake. He can talk your language. You'll understand my situation if you talk with him," she told the officers.

"Mr. Brambly? We know him well," the officer told Cathy, and he moved a telephone over to where she sat at the desk.

Cathy rummaged through her handbag to find Brambly's contact information. She couldn't find it and was getting more and more frustrated as she searched. The officer left the room for a moment, and when she returned, handed Cathy the number for Private Investigator Brambly. Cathy took the number and dialed.

"Hello," answered Brambly.

"Mr. Brambly, its Cathy Dimmer. I need your help. Can you come to the NYPD headquarters now?"

"NYPD headquarters? What happened?" he asked.

"Jake and I got into a nasty fight, and I called 911 for help," she answered.

"I'll be there in fifteen minutes," he told her.

Cathy exhaled a big sigh of relief and turned to tell the officer that the investigator would arrive in fifteen minutes. Then she had second thoughts. What if having Jake investigated made her look jealous? That would play into Jake's story. She decided to take her chances that the investigation findings would speak for themselves.

Brambly arrived as scheduled and joined Cathy at the officer's desk. He was carrying a large brown envelope as he pulled up another chair.

"Hello, Mary," he said to the officer. Then he turned to Cathy. "Nice to see you, Mrs. Dimmer." He asked Officer Stillman, "What on earth is going on?"

"We have a domestic dispute, with opposing stories of the event," Officer Mary Stillman answered.

"Cathy, what happened?" Brambly asked.

Cathy explained the sequence of events that led up to the tussle in their penthouse apartment a few hours earlier. She was noticeably shaken by the review of events and started to cry.

Brambly reached into his pocket, pulled out a handkerchief for her, and handed it to her. Cathy took it and dabbed her eyes while taking a deep breath to regain her composure.

"Officer, if Mrs. Dimmer agrees to share the findings of a recent investigation into her husband's secret life, I have brought pictures for you to see," Brambly told the officer. Cathy gave a nod of consent.

The officers agreed to look at the photos that Brambly had spread onto the surface of the desk. Cathy looked away, trying to avoid any more emotional pain.

"This investigation unearthed Jake's other life, which was unknown to his wife. In fact, I just gave Mrs. Dimmer the report earlier today. The reality of living with a stranger clearly caused Cathy to want a divorce. It is my belief that Jake will do anything to prevent a divorce and the loss of his lucrative lifestyle," Brambly explained.

The officers shook their heads as they looked at the photos and listened to Brambly's report. They had respect for Investigator Brambly and did not doubt his story.

"It's time we confront Jake with this evidence and get him to revise his story," the officer told them. "In the meantime, Mrs. Dimmer, you can begin the request for a restraining order from the judge." The officer gave Cathy a complaint form to fill out. Brambly leaned over toward Cathy to assist her in completing the form. The officers left to join Officer Harry Means, who was questioning Jake Dimmer in a nearby room.

Officer Stillman called Officer Means out of the room. "Harry, you need to see what Brambly has shown me regarding Mr. Dimmer. It certainly helped me to see Mrs. Dimmer's side of the story," she told him as they made their way back to Stillman's desk and the telling photo gallery on it.

"Oh, man," commented Officer Means as he looked at the photos. "It seems like you have him dead to rights on this. No wonder he lost it," Means commented.

Brambly interrupted. "Jake hasn't seen these photos yet, sir! He has no idea that Cathy hired me to investigate him," he added as the two officers listened.

Officer Means said, "So his life is about to come down around him when you file for a restraining order and make public the reason for your request for a divorce."

"I feared for my life. What else could I do?" Cathy asked.

Officer Stillman quickly stepped in. "We're so sorry. This must be really difficult for you."

"Yes, it is difficult to see your life torn to bits," Cathy whispered.

Brambly stepped toward Cathy and put his arm around her shoulders to console her. Brambly ran through the choices presented to Cathy. Should they confront Jake? Should they file the complaint? Was it time for the Dimmers to face each other? Was it time to charge Jake with domestic disturbance? With no hard evidence, this would not be a good idea. It was her word against his. Only Brambly's evidence might shock Jake into an agreement to give Cathy space, to stay away from her.

Brambly left Cathy and joined the officers in the interrogation room. He took a moment with them to explain that this incident was just one of several other incidents involving Jake being investigated by the FBI. He said that there was more to this story. He told them that they should probably inform the FBI of this situation and that the FBI already had the photos. They agreed to call the FBI agents, Curley and Stewart that Brambly had met in the Cayman Islands.

Chapter 22

A FLURRY OF TEXT MESSAGES FLEW between Investigator Brambly, Agents Stewart and Curley, and Bud and Rosa. *"Jake Dimmer currently being questioned in police station regarding domestic disturbance and two 911 calls from his wife."*

Bud and Rosa were on their way to the Dimmers' penthouse when they got the text message. They changed direction and headed to the police station.

They entered the station, identified themselves, and asked the officer in charge to find the location of the Dimmers.

"Officers Stillman and Means are with Mrs. Dimmer and Investigator Brambly in the conference room. Mr. Dimmer is waiting in a separate area at the moment," the office told Bud and Rosa.

"Thank you," Rosa said, and she and Bud found their way to the conference room.

As they entered, they saw that the group—Officers Stillman and Means, Agents Curley and Stewart, Investigator Brambly, and Mrs. Dimmer—were assembled around a long table in the conference room They heard Officer Means suggest they move to another room holding Jake Dimmer. Rosa and Bud waved and called, "Can we have a word before you go in there?" The group paused before proceeding and looked at Bud and Rosa.

Officer Stillman spoke first. "Nice to see you, Bud, Rosa. We are about to confront Jake with the findings of an investigation done by Mr. Brambly. Seems like this might help Mr. Dimmer come to his senses. Reality check as it were," she told them.

"The FBI would like to be part of this discussion," Bud told the officers.

"Join us then," Means said as the officers picked up their papers and headed for the door. Down the hall they entered the room where Jake had been waiting. Cathy waited in the observation room while the other officers went to talk with Jake.

Jake remained defiant during the beginning of the meeting with Officers Stillman and Means, Bud and Rosa, Investigator Brambly and agents Stewart and Curley.

"What the hell is this, a convention?" Jake demanded, looking around at the seven seated questioners.

"No, Mr. Dimmer, this is your life," Means snapped.

"Listen, charge me or let me go!" Jake demanded.

"Mr. Dimmer, we have something to show you. Are you interested?" Officer Stillman asked.

"Shouldn't I have my lawyer here?" he asked.

"Sir, that is up to you. Is that what you want?" Means asked.

Jake thought for a moment. "No. What do you have for me to see? Besides, I thought that this was about the false accusations brought against me by my wife. Do you now have some trumped-up photos of a black eye?" he said with a smirk.

"Sir, your wife is filing a formal complaint and is asking for a restraining order against you," Officer Stillman replied.

"She is lying. I never touched her. She kicked me. Maybe I should file a restraining order against her," he snapped back.

"That is your right," Means told him. "But first, I would suggest that you look at the photos," he said, pushing a folder across the table.

Jake felt his knee jerk and his bravado vanished as he glanced at the open folder of photographs of him with a variety of young men in very compromising positions.

"Holy shit!" he whispered, holding his head. "Where did you get these fake photos?" he asked.

"Mr. Dimmer, these photos are authentic, every one of them," answered Investigator Brambly. "You see, Mr. Dimmer, I was hired by your wife to find out where all your travels took you. She became concerned that you were not being honest with her. She thought that you had a mistress. When the FBI questioned both of you, she noticed that your stories varied from what you had told her. I gave her my report this morning with the photos. She is still in shock."

"I want my lawyer!" Jake demanded, and that ended the session with the police until his lawyer could come to a meeting with him. The group dispersed, leaving Jake in the room to call his lawyer and Cathy still watching from the observation room. She heard Jake on the telephone.

"Listen, you need to get over here right now. They are getting ready to put together some trumped-up charges about domestic disturbance, a restraining order, and god knows what else. This is all made up by Cathy to make me look like a monster … No, I don't want to hear a word from you. Get over here now. Hurry!"

"The noose is getting tighter and tighter around Jake's neck, I'd say," Rosa told Bud as they stood next to Cathy in the observation room looking through the one-way glass as Jake contacted his lawyer.

"It is only a matter of time now until we put all the pieces together on warrants for his arrest for the attempted murder of his brother and for the murder of Arthur Milne," Bud added.

"This is the first I'm hearing about murder or attempted murder," Cathy said in disbelief.

"Domestic disturbance is the least of his problems. He must be feeling the heat," Rosa surmised.

It took less than thirty minutes until Jake's lawyer arrived; it was Cathy's family lawyer, Roger Milburne of Roger Milburne Associates.

****

Detective Sylvia Santos texted Bud Black the latest findings in the long-awaited forensic report. She told him that two different semen samples were identified, the presence of alcohol and oxycodone were confirmed, and DNA from under the victim's nails was available for a match. She asked if he had a DNA sample from the person of interest.

Officer Santos sat back in her chair in the Provincetown Police station and picked up the folder on the lighthouse murder to review it again.

As she read, she made a mental note of each finding. A young man was strangled with a belt. A second male was present and left semen on the victim. Neighbors were able to give the police information regarding an SUV and enough information for the police sketch artist to make a likeness of the visitor. Several items were recovered at the victim's apartment belonging to a visitor. Sylvia noted that the identical twins were both persons of interest and lived in New York City. The summary also had Bud's findings in New York City and in Provincetown. She thought, *if Bud gets DNA from the suspect and it is a match, we're golden.* Then she realized that identical twins shared the same gene pool. That complicated things. Even in a lineup of identical twins, how would the guilty twin be identified?

Sylvia received a text message from Bud. *"Nice to hear from you. Timing couldn't be better. Presently waiting for lawyer before continuing questioning of prime suspect. DNA has been gathered on a cup used a few minutes ago by suspect at police station. Search warrants requested for Dimmer penthouse. More as soon as I can. Bud."*

Sylvia continued reading through the lighthouse murder file folder. She realized that this was not a slam-dunk case. It was fraught with twists and turns. Identical twins complicated things. They had to have an airtight case before they could go to the next step of filing a murder charge. *Where would the crime be tried, Massachusetts or New York?* she wondered. *The murder occurred in Massachusetts, Barnstable County. The suspect lives in New York, but committed the crime here. Even if he is arrested in New York, he'd have to face a Massachusetts court, where there is no death penalty.* Her mind wove in and out from present facts to future unknowns. The FBI's involvement could trump the state, and there was the possibility they might take over and move the case to federal court, since violent death and drugs were both major players in the investigation. No matter what happened, the Provincetown Police Department was ready and able to do their part in order to bring justice to the victim and his family. Sylvia was still trying to track down the victim's relatives, with little luck so far. She vowed to find someone who cared about the young man named Arthur Milne, relative or not.

Chapter 23

THE POLICE CHIEF, BUD AND Rosa, Jake Dimmer, and his lawyer assembled around a table in the conference room. Cathy Dimmer and two FBI agents, Curley and Stewart, observed through a one-way mirror in the adjoining room.

The lawyer, Roger Milburne, nodded that the questioning of Jake Dimmer, his client, could continue in his presence. Jake sat smugly next to his lawyer, having no idea that his wife was watching. The lawyer had taken time to look through the photos and had talked briefly with an irate Jake.

"We want everyone to understand that this domestic disturbance charge is only the tip of the iceberg. Apart from his wife's formal complaint and her request for a restraining order against your client, the FBI, working with the Provincetown and New York City police, have had Mr. Dimmer under surveillance for some time now. He is the prime suspect in a murder case and drug trafficking," FBI Agent Bud Black told them.

"Garbage, lies, frame-up," Jake spit out uncontrollably as his lawyer pressed his arm to quiet him. But Jake continued his tirade. "You have no proof that I've done anything wrong. The photos are Photoshop fakes," he yelled.

"I think that you need to arrest my client or let him go," Attorney Milburne responded to all three of the law enforcement officers present once Jake stopped yelling.

"Are you *crazy?*" Jake confronted his lawyer. "I'm not guilty of anything. Why would you tell them to arrest me?"

"Jake, calm down. They are making very serious charges, and if they have a case they need to do more than threaten you," Roger told him sternly. "Keep quiet. You are not helping yourself with these outbursts."

Jake had defiance written all over his reddened face.

"If your client would admit his guilt, we would consider manslaughter instead of premeditated murder," Bud suggested.

"Premeditated murder? Get serious! Accidents happen," Jake spurted out to the horror of his attorney and Cathy, still watching from the observation room.

"Jake, don't say another word! Do you hear me?" insisted his attorney.

Jake slouched down in his chair. He had said something he hadn't meant to say.

"You are right. Accidents do happen, Jake. Can you tell us how it happened?" Rosa asked.

"Jake, we need to talk," the attorney told Jake before he answered.

But Jake's arrogance wouldn't let him be silent. "I know what I'm doing. I'm innocent," he snapped back at his attorney.

"Do you mind if we record what you are about to say, Jake?" Rosa asked.

"I have nothing to hide, and I don't mind," he answered her.

His attorney was unable to get Jake's attention as the story Jake fantasized began.

"Some of you know that I am an identical twin. Jimmy is my younger brother by a few minutes. He is a dentist, lives alone, and frequents Provincetown. The photos you showed me may have been Jimmy. If he killed somebody, you need to nab him, not me. He was always in trouble growing up. We used to be very close, but I haven't seen or talked with him in some time." Jake's momentum was picking up as he continued lying. He had years of practice. He believed what he was saying, and he was convincing. "Have you talked with Jimmy yet?" Jake asked.

"Jake, we would rather hear your whole story. Keep going," Rosa said.

"Sure. I heard that you found a few of Jimmy's things in an apartment in Provincetown. Is that right?" Jake asked.

"Where did you hear that, Jake?" asked Bud.

"You told me," he answered, even fabricating this angle.

"Did I tell you where I found these items you say I found?" Bud baited the cocky liar.

"You found the bathing shorts in the bedroom closet, and the gold chain in the top drawer of the dresser," he answered, feeling very confident.

"Are you sure that you want to continue talking, Jake?" Roger Milburne asked his disobedient client.

Again, Jake shrugged his attorney off, and continued his story.

"Jake, are you aware of the 'accident' we are talking about?" Rosa asked.

"Some gay guy got killed in Provincetown the Friday night I was in Philadelphia on business," he answered flippantly.

"Who told you that the victim was gay?" Bud asked. "Who told you that the victim was killed Friday night?"

"Well, he was, wasn't he?" Jake snapped back.

"Jake, how was he killed?" Rosa asked.

"I read in the news that a belt got stuck around his neck and he suffocated."

At that comment, Bud knocked on the mirror for the agents to join them in the conference room.

"Jake Dimmer, you are under arrest for the murder of Arthur Milne." He read Jake his Miranda rights and nodded to the police in the room to take him into custody for processing. "It is my job to return you to Massachusetts," Bud continued.

"Wait, you've got this all wrong. I'm innocent! Jimmy did it!" he screamed. "What am I paying you for, Roger?" Jake shouted angrily as the officers took him out of the room in handcuffs. He looked helplessly at his attorney, who bent his head down and glanced away.

Rosa left the room to join Cathy, who had remained in the observation room.

Cathy Dimmer swooned and sat down, finding the whole experience overwhelming. Agent Stewart assisted her to a chair in the observation room. Rosa went for some water and a compress for Cathy's head.

"In trying to frame his twin brother, Jake incriminated himself in the murder. He told us things about the murder that only the murderer would know. Details about the murder have not been released to the press. He has no idea how much evidence we have on him for the murder in Provincetown, as well as the attempted murder of his brother,

Jimmy. Jake is in deep trouble," Rosa told Cathy Dimmer. "He will be offered bail while he waits for arraignment. Will you post bail for him?"

"*No!* I had no idea. I had no idea," Cathy repeated, wiping her eyes and looking away into space. Agents Stewart and Curely talked with Bud before they finished their part of the assignment.

"Can I have someone take you home?" Rosa asked.

"Yes, I don't feel strong enough to drive," Cathy told her.

Rosa called to Curley and Stewart for this job. Agent Stewart offered his assistance right away. "At your service," he announced, trying to remain serious but obviously delighted to drive her home.

It had been a trying day for Cathy Dimmer. There was the Brambly report, the questioning, the physical fight with Jake, her own filing of a complaint, and Jake's arrogance and uncontrolled talking that got him arrested. She needed to be alone.

Chapter 24

BUD AND ROSA ARRIVED IN Provincetown to talk with Detective Santos after delivering Jake Dimmer to the Massachusetts State Police in Middleborough. They wanted to be sure that the case file was complete and that no loose ends remained. They updated Detective Santos on the arrest of Jake Dimmer, his return to Barnstable County, and the beginning of the long process leading up to the criminal trial, unless he took a plea.

In Provincetown the rumor swirled around.

"Did ja hear they got the sucka that killed the waiter?" a local Provincetown man was saying to his friend, the shopkeeper. Both were standing at the entrance facing Commercial Street.

"No! Was it a fight? Booze? Drugs?" the storekeeper asked.

"Nobody ain't sayin yet," he answered, showing his concern by nervously stepping on and off the curb and wringing his hands that such a terrible thing had happened in his town.

"I'll bet they have the bastard dead to rights," the shopkeeper added.

"Yup, you can't fool around with our police. They'll get ja," he agreed.

A town police car drove by the two men, and the policeman inside rolled down the patrol car window, waved, and said, "Hi Guys." The two waved back with big grins. They respected their police department for all the work they did to keep order in the town, especially in the summer.

At the police station, Rosa and Bud were busily going over the case with Detective Sylvia Santos in the detective's area of the building.

"Are there any missing pieces to this murder case?" Bud asked.

"We have the forensic report tying the DNA samples to both Jake and the victim, Arthur Milne. We have DNA matches of Arthur and Jake on Jake's belt. By the way, thanks for securing the belt in the house search, and the DNA samples from Jake's cup during questioning in the New York police station," Detective Santos said.

"No problem," Bud responded.

"We have the affidavit from Arthur's employer identifying Jake, Jake's silver SUV, and his frequent visits to pick Arthur up at work," she added.

"We have identified Jimmy, Jake's twin, on the whale watch the day of the murder. It is not a good alibi against Jake's accusations. The time window of the death according to the examiner's report is early evening to midnight. We need to find out where Jimmy was that evening," Bud told the detective. Bud added a written report of that part of the investigation into the case file.

"A very disturbing aspect of this case is that we now have evidence from Jake's doctor regarding a prescription of the drug that Jake used to try to kill his brother and make it look like suicide. He wanted us to believe that his brother's guilt drove him to take an overdose. We believe that Jake's world is coming down around him, and he wanted to free himself by framing his twin. Can you imagine such a thing?" Rosa told the detective.

"Is the attempted murder charge being filed in New York?" Detective Santos asked.

"Yes," Bud replied.

"What about Jake's wife in all of this?" Detective Santos asked.

"She has filed for divorce and moved from the penthouse apartment to be with her family in Scarsdale, New York."

"This was really difficult for her. She thought that Jake had a mistress. Just think of the shock of finding out that he likes young men," Rosa added.

"We have the swim shorts and the gold chain in the evidence bags," the detective added, steering the conversation back to the murder case.

"That may be tricky. We need to prove that Jake planted the items that belonged to Jimmy in Milne's apartment," said Bud, looking at Rosa and Sylvia.

"Jimmy has told us that he left the items in Jake's car glove compartment," Rosa added, "giving Jake ample access to the items."

"Does Jake have a good lawyer?" the detective asked out of curiosity.

"You know, I'm not sure. The family attorney has no obligation to take the case, considering how poorly Jake treated him before he was arrested. Also, with Cathy divorcing Jake, Jake is probably on his own in this mess," chimed Rosa.

"Massachusetts will appoint a lawyer to him if he needs one. Does he know that?" Sylvia asked. "For that to happen, Jake will be held in our state, where he will be tried for the murder of Arthur Milne," she added. "Yesterday I found a cousin of Arthur's, who came to identify his body. She said that the family disowned him years ago. Very sad," she told Bud.

"New York has fully cooperated in extraditing Jake from New York to Massachusetts," Bud said. "We handed him over a couple of hours ago to the state police in Middleborough."

"The New York City chief of police, Guy Fox, a dear friend of mine, has assured us of their cooperation," Rosa agreed. "The process will go smoothly."

"Bud, what does the FBI have in store for you next?" Detective Santos asked as their meeting was coming to a close.

"I'll return to RAID and wait for the next FBI special assignment while I'm working there," he said, looking directly at Rosa. "Of course, if this case gets to trial, I'll be a witness for the prosecution," he added.

"We look forward to his return," Rosa said.

"We'll miss you, Bud. We don't always have the state police and FBI involved in our cases. Of course, we rarely have murders. You guys have the labs and support for us. I hope that you'll keep in touch." Detective Santos gave Bud a good-bye hug, then extended her friendliness in a good-bye hug to Rosa.

Just as the three were heading for the door, Detective Santos received a telephone call from the NYPD. "This is Chief Fox, Detective Santos. I have just had word from the Massachusetts State Police that Jake Dimmer was beaten badly in lockup. I'll keep you in the loop as to his condition. You do realize that he has to be returned to New York, where he is charged with attempted murder, in good condition!" he told her.

"Yes, I understand. Thanks, Chief."

The detective relayed the news to the others. The three stood in silent shock; it was not how they wanted things to turn out.

Chapter 25

BUD AND ROSA LEFT THE Provincetown Police station and traveled to the Massachusetts State Police Middleborough lockup, where they had left Jake Dimmer several hours before.

"What the hell happened to Jake Dimmer?" Bud demanded of the officer in charge when they arrived.

"We were as surprised as you are, sir. He was being held in a cell by himself. No one beat him up. He threw himself around in the cell hitting the walls as hard as he could, according to the videotape and the report we got from the officer who found him," the police officer told Bud and Rosa.

"Where is he?" asked Rosa.

"He is in our infirmary. He's sedated and not communicative."

"When can we see him?" Bud asked.

"Probably in a few days," he answered.

"That is not good enough. We need to see him now!" Bud demanded.

The officer thought for a few moments. "Follow me," he told them.

The two followed the officer to the infirmary, where Jake had been treated for abrasions, cuts, and bruises, along with a fractured shoulder. His eyes were closed. His head was bandaged, and his shoulder was taped and supported with an arm sling.

As they stood by the bed observing Jake's physical state, he opened his swollen eyes and looked at them.

"Can you hear me?" Rosa asked him.

"Yesh," he slurred slowly.

"Why did you throw yourself against the cell walls?" she asked.

Jake struggled to speak coherently. "They beat me," he was able to get out. "I want a lawyer."

"Who is your lawyer, Jake?" Rosa asked.

"We'll need his name and contact information," Bud added.

Jake fell into a deep sleep and did not answer.

"I'll call Cathy Dimmer for information regarding a lawyer for Jake. In the meantime, we need to be concerned that he is setting himself up for a mental health defense when he can't prove that the guards beat him," Rosa suggested.

"He will have no chance to prove abuse by the police. Every cell is monitored by video camera. They are able to show him thrashing around the cell to get the injuries he is being treated for in the infirmary," Bud said to the on-duty officer.

"That's right. We monitor every cell. We have him on tape running full speed into the wall several times before our office got to him," the officer told Bud and Rosa.

"Jake doesn't know that fact yet, so he'll be telling another story," Rosa suggested.

Bud called Guy Fox at the NYPD explaining what they had found out regarding Jake Dimmer's self-inflicted injuries.

Rosa called Cathy Dimmer trying to get information regarding a lawyer for Jake.

"Thanks for the update," Cathy was saying. "He is on his own. As far as I know, he is penniless—unless he has drug money stashed away someplace. Our family attorney will not take his case," she told Rosa.

"Should we proceed with a request for a public defender?" Rosa asked.

"I really don't care what you do," Cathy Dimmer said strongly. "Please don't contact me again about this. You can talk to me through my attorney, Mr. Milburne. Good-bye."

"We have a problem," she announced to Bud. "Jake is on his own for legal services."

"Which court is going to try his case? When we find out, we'll alert the judge to assign a public defender for him," Bud told Rosa and the officer standing there.

"I'll see to this first thing in the morning. I take it that the state of Massachusetts is going to bring charges against him for murder?" the officer asked.

"The FBI wants this to go to federal court, where we can bring him up on a first-degree murder charge and drug trafficking," Bud answered.

"Until we have the paperwork for that, I'll file the case at the Barnstable County Courthouse in Massachusetts, in the county where the murder occurred," the officer told him. "Where can I reach you to give you an update?" he asked.

Bud provided the officer with his FBI business card with his cell phone information. The officer put the card on top of his clipboard with Jake Dimmer's intake information and photo.

Jake Dimmer was proving to be a major challenge. The authorities had to keep him safe, get him a public defender, and get him to the state courthouse for a hearing in one piece. They needed to have around-the-clock security to watch him and protect him from himself and any other self-inflicted injuries he might attempt. Sedating him was a short-term fix in the first days in the infirmary. The authorities were considering a suicide watch or transferring him to a secure mental health facility within the Massachusetts prison system until he could be moved to the holding cell in Barnstable County. Their decision would depend on the results of a mental health report by their own state psychiatrist, who would examine him as soon as he was coherent.

Chapter 26

JIMMY DIMMER'S ATTORNEY, BARRY SILVERSMITH, was talking to his client in the hospital room about the circumstances that brought Jim there. He was telling Jimmy that his brother was being accused of attempted murder because he overdosed him with a drug called doxepin. He asked if Jim understood. Jimmy nodded yes.

"You will soon be able to leave the hospital. It was a close call for you. You almost died," Barry told him.

"The police were here. They want me to work for the prosecution on this. I can't do that. Jake is my brother," he told the attorney.

"Are you a total fool? He tried to kill you." Silversmith stood up from the chair by Jimmy's bed and paced the room.

"He's my flesh and blood," Jimmy insisted. "He may have problems, but he is not evil."

"Jimmy, you need to know that Jake is dangerous to himself and others. He needs help. You can help the authorities understand that. Work with them," the attorney pleaded.

"Is that true? Can they help him?" Jimmy asked.

"Yes. But you have to help them. Jake is in Massachusetts now facing a first-degree murder charge. He will be returned to New York eventually to face the attempted murder charge on you. This is very serious. Please consider cooperating with the authorities. You realize that you will be brought into the Massachusetts case. Jake has accused you of the murder. He has said that you ran and attempted suicide because of your guilt. The evidence does not support that, luckily for you. Jake accused you! Do you hear me?" Barry asked.

"I'll think about all you've told me, Barry. I promise."

"You know that I will work for you and do whatever I can to clear your name in this," Barry told him. "I have a report here from the detective I hired to track Jake. It is very damning information, Jim. Your brother has another life, one he spends in gay bars with young men. The FBI suspects him of drug trafficking, because of his undocumented wealth. They are searching for offshore accounts."

"Do you believe that bullshit? My brother is *not* gay!" he shouted.

"I believe the report, the photographs, and the corroborating information from the FBI files."

"Let me see them!" Jim demanded. Barry handed Jim the folder, and he opened it.

Shock spilled across his face. He looked at the photographs over and over. He ran his hands through his hair and wiped his unbelieving eyes on his shirt sleeves. When he had had enough, he returned the folder to the attorney.

"You need to leave me now," he whispered to Barry.

Silversmith said good-bye, gathered his papers and the folder of Jake's indiscretions, and left Jim to ponder what he had just learned. It was all too much to bear for Jimmy. He was trying to wrap his mind around the whole messy situation with Jake. He was trying to believe what was happening to him and to Jake. Exhausted from Barry's visit, he needed to rest before he could think.

*****

Later that afternoon, Bud and Rosa arrived at Jimmy Dimmer's hospital room. Jimmy was sitting in a chair by the window reading.

"How are you feeling, Dr. Dimmer?" Rosa asked. She was no longer in disguise as a coed and was prepared to explain her charade to him if he recognized her. He didn't.

"Hello. Not bad. Thanks for asking. I'm leaving tomorrow, they tell me."

"Are you aware that your brother was arrested for murder?" Bud asked.

"Yes, my attorney told me earlier today," he answered.

"I'm sorry about his injuries," Rosa added.

"What injuries?" Jimmy asked, perking up.

"Your bother flung himself against the cell walls and caused some broken bones and head abrasions last night," Rosa continued. "He's in the infirmary, where they have sedated him."

"How serious is it? Can I see him? Did the guards beat him? Sounds like the guards beat him," Jimmy said.

"No, Jake did all the damage by himself," Bud reported.

"How do you know? Maybe his cellmate beat him up," Jimmy said.

"No. His injuries were all self-inflicted and recorded on video surveillance cameras. He was in the cell alone," Rosa said.

Jimmy Dimmer started to cry. He wanted to get his brother help. He would get his brother help. Things were not going well for Jake. He was in deep trouble. The reality was overwhelming for Jimmy.

"I have to see Jake. I'll know what to do. This is all a mistake!"

"Dr. Dimmer, you are going to be summoned to court if this case goes to trial. We want you to be honest with the jury. We believe that you are innocent, but a jury does not know what we know. Jake's attorney will try to establish doubt in the mind of the jury regarding you. Although we have solid evidence against Jake, he will try to beat the system. He is trying to implicate you," Rosa told Jim. "Being an identical twin at this point may cause a major problem identifying the guilty twin. Do you understand?" she continued.

"Jake needs help, not jail. My attorney said that medical help was possible if I work with you. Is that true?" Jim asked.

"Yes," Bud answered. "Your participation may lead to a deal, avoiding a trial."

"You mean I can keep Jake out of jail?" the twin asked.

"Let's put it this way: Jake could spend time in a secure hospital as part of the deal. That is, if he admits to the murder," Bud told the dentist. "Freedom may elude him."

"Then what kind of deal is that?" Jimmy asked.

"It will save Jake from the death penalty. It will spare him and could get him the mental health attention he may need," Rosa added.

"So I give him up to save his life?" Jimmy asked, somewhat befuddled.

"Something like that. You are also saving your own skin from Jake's accusations that you are the murderer," Bud explained.

"I thought you said that the evidence doesn't support that accusation," Jim persisted.

"Juries are funny. Things can go wrong. The unknown here is that you are identical twins. Jake could make a convincing case that we have the wrong man, that he is the innocent one," Rosa added.

"Then I could say the same thing. Who are they going to convict? I think that we'll both walk," Jim proposed.

"Or you'll both go to prison, because one of you committed this crime," Bud said. "Do you want to go to prison for a murder you had nothing to do with on that fatal weekend?"

The room fell silent, and Jimmy Dimmer was hit by the reality of what was happening to him. He finally understood that there was no way out of this. He decided to cooperate. He agreed to a deal to help his brother while helping himself. He understood.

Chapter 27

JAKE WAS TAKEN TO A quiet room near the infirmary to meet with the state psychiatrist. He was in his usual take on the world mood. Jake believed his own stories as though they were true, and no one could convince him otherwise. He was looking forward to the meeting with Dr. Frick. In his mind, this was just one more bit of evidence to support his claims of innocence.

"Good morning, Jake," the doctor said to him as he came into the room. He sat down on the chair provided near Jake.

"Is it?" Jake snapped, being a bit cocky.

"Do you know why you are here?" The doctor addressed Jake gently.

"Of course I do, to talk with you," he answered, giving himself another point in his imaginary game.

"That's right, to talk with me and to answer some questions. Is that okay with you?" the doctor asked.

"Go for it. I've been looking forward to this," Jake told Dr. Frick.

"Bear with me. Some of these questions may seem silly," the doctor told him before they began. "What is your name?" he asked.

"Jake Dimmer, and I'm an identical twin, the older by a few minutes," Jake told the doctor.

"Jake, just answer the question. Try not to add information not asked for," the doctor told him. "Where do you live?"

"With my wife in a penthouse at Seventy-Ninth and Park Avenue, New York City," he answered.

"What do you do for a living?"

"Is this confidential?" Jake asked the doctor.

"Yes."

"I'm a secret agent," he said.

"Who do you work for?"

"That's a secret." Jake laughed.

"I was told that you were in sales. Is that wrong?" Dr. Frick continued.

"Not exactly wrong," Jake responded.

"Can you explain that?"

"I deal in secret things of great value, hence, my wealth," he answered.

"Jake, do you love your twin brother?"

"Of course I do," he snapped again.

"Which of you is the favorite of your mother?" The doctor believed that this question could trigger a raw nerve in Jake and get him to open up with more honesty.

"He is, the little turd," he hissed. "Don't ask me why. He is only a dentist, and I'm rich," he chanted.

"Is being rich important to you?"

"Isn't it important to you?" Jake asked.

"Try to answer the question for me," the doctor advised without responding to Jake's question.

"Yes, it is important. I came from the projects in New York, and I am not going back," he exploded.

"Tell me about your married life to Cathy Astor Dimmer," Dr. Frick asked.

"We have the best marriage possible. We never fight. We have great sex. She loves me and would never leave me. She is always home waiting with open arms for me when I come home from a business trip. We want to start a family soon." Jake seemed to be dreaming out loud, not even aware that he was not being honest regarding a pending divorce.

"Do you go on many business trips?"

"Not too many," he lied.

"Do you want to talk about your secret life?"

Jake was dumbfounded with the question. What did the doctor know about his secret life? Who told him? Was this a trap? Jake's paranoia was alive and well, and this question triggered his defense.

"I told you that I cannot talk about my work." He skirted the real question.

"If you could talk about your secret to someone, would that make you feel better?"

Jake was very uncomfortable. He knew that the doctor was not talking about his work. He fidgeted in his chair and showed a lip twitch. He thought of Arthur lying on the beach, never to wake up. How he wanted Arthur to wake up! He felt sick. He was suddenly very pale.

"I can't go on with this meeting now. I don't feel well," he told the doctor.

"I'm sorry if the last question upset you. Sometimes it is a burden to carry a secret. Are you sure that you don't want to get it off your mind?"

"My brother killed his lover!" he blurted out and began to cry.

"How do you know that?"

Gathering himself together and wiping the tears from his face on his sleeves, Jake looked at the doctor. "He told me the other day when he visited," he lied.

"Have you told anyone else this secret?"

"Indirectly," he answered.

"Can you explain that?"

"Well, I told the police that my brother was in Provincetown the weekend of the incident, not me. They found items of clothing that belong to my brother in the apartment of the dead man. The evidence points to my brother. To top it off, he is gay, and they have photos to prove it. The problem is that we are identical twins, and they think that I'm the one in the photos they showed him." Jake continued to portray himself as unfairly accused.

"So you have told the police this story?"

"I've tried. They don't want to hear it."

"You said that you love your brother. If he is guilty, he could get the death penalty. Do you know that?"

"There is where you are wrong. The crime was committed in Massachusetts, where there is no death penalty. Besides, this was at best manslaughter, accidental, not planned." He began to open up, mixing known information with information not given to anyone.

"Can you explain that?"

"Everyone knows how gays fool around, use drugs, and play sex games. Well, duh, that's what happened, drugs and an accident," he continued, feeling safe that the doctor had said this conversation was confidential.

"As an identical twin, do you understand how your brother felt about this person whom you say he accidentally killed?" The doctor gambled that this question would trigger transference from blaming his brother to Jake's own feelings.

"He loved him very much. He loved him more than he had ever loved anyone in his whole life. He had found a soul mate. He wanted to be with him every minute and every hour. He traveled to be with him every week. He wanted to marry him." Jake was crying as he confessed his own secret. He had lost the man he loved. "He didn't mean it. It was an accident. He didn't mean it." He cried uncontrollably.

The doctor gave Jake a moment to calm himself. "Jake, can you own your own secret? Was it you who lost everything when Arthur died in your arms?"

"Yes, yes, yes," he sobbed, burying his head in his arms on the table.

The doctor believed that Jake was in control of his faculties, knew what had happened, and lied whenever it was to his advantage. It would be impossible to mount an insanity defense. He was sane, and Frick's examination report would declare it. Dr. Frick would suggest that this was not murder, but an accidental death, unplanned and unexpected. Framing his twin for the crime was consistent with Jake's egocentric personality, chronic lying, and drive for self-preservation, but not insanity. Dr. Frick wrote his report with a sentence that would explain Jake's psychological diagnosis.

The patient exhibits sociopathic behavior, with the lack of a moral compass.

In addition to the hard evidence the police had, this examination would give them the "why" of the crime. It would be up to the authorities how they would proceed with the case.

Chapter 28

SEVERAL DAYS HAD GONE BY since Jimmy Dimmer had been released from the hospital. He had decided to visit with his mother on his way to his apartment in New York City. He tried to console her and explain that things would work out and not to worry. He tried to be convincing, but he was never able to be as convincing as Jake was. At least, he was honest.

"What made you sick, Jimmy?" his mother wanted to know.

"Nothing, Mom, kind of a flu," he told her.

"Honey, don't lie to me. What happened?" she insisted.

"The doctor said I had a drug overdose."

"But you don't take drugs, do you, sweetheart?" she pressed.

"No, Mom, I don't take drugs." Which begged the next question from his mother.

"Then how did you have a drug overdose?"

"The authorities believe that Jake gave it to me in the tea," he told her.

"Well, now, I've heard everything! That is ridiculous!! Why would he do such a mean thing to you?"

"I don't know, but I am going to visit him and find out."

As soon as Jimmy got home, he called his attorney. "I need to see Jake."

"I'm doing what I can to arrange the meeting. The prison officials tell me that Jake is still not able to receive visitors. As soon as he can, I'll be notified," Barry told Jim.

"That is not good enough. I'm family, and I want to see him now." Jim had become agitated.

"I hear you. I understand your frustration. I'm doing what I can to get you in to see your brother," Barry told him again.

Jimmy slammed down the telephone. He was not satisfied. Then he remembered the coed, Maria. He remembered what a nice time they had had at the jazz jam session. Maybe she could help him somehow. At least she could listen to his plight. He had no idea how to contact her.

When Rosa heard that Jimmy had been released from the hospital, she phoned him.

"It's Maria, I hope that you remember me from the jazz club. Please call me I need to talk with you," she left her number on his answering machine and hung up.

Rosa was busy finishing up recording the last pieces of evidence in the murder case from the Dimmer house search when her cell phone vibrated in her pocket. She checked the call. Oh yes, it was Jimmy Dimmer returning her call. It was time to be honest with him. *No more coed, no more Maria, no more lies*, she thought.

Rosa called from her desk to Bud's in the busy precinct room.

"Bud, I have a call from Jimmy Dimmer. I'll see him before I leave for DC tomorrow. He sounded a bit desperate," Rosa told him.

"I can't believe that your vacation, or should I say your working holiday, is over. I have enjoyed your visit so much," Bud told her. "Thanks for all the help on this case. I think we have it ready for a successful prosecution," he added. "Let me know if I can help with Jimmy."

"I'll be glad when you are back at RAID. We have an unbelievable caseload, and I could use your help. I've had a wonderful time," Rosa told him. She got up from behind her desk and gave him a hug and peck on the cheek. She left Bud's and her temporary work space at the NYPD to go to Guy's office to say good-bye to Guy. Next she called Jimmy Dimmer.

"Hello, Jimmy here, I got your call," Rosa heard Jimmy's voice say.

"Hi. I was afraid that you would not remember me. If you did remember me, you'd be mad at me for breaking our lunch date so abruptly. I'm really sorry about that, but I had to visit my mother," he told her.

"Actually, I need to talk to you too," Rosa told him. "Can we meet this afternoon?"

"Yes. I'd like that. Do you want to meet at the jazz club?" he asked.

"Is it open?" Rosa asked as she looked at her watch; it was nearing four in the afternoon.

"I can meet you there at five, and yes, it is open. There will be a jam session later tonight," he told her.

"I'll be there," Rosa told him as the call ended. She let out a big sigh, not knowing how he was going to take the surprise that was coming his way.

Rosa's things were in Bud's car. She was going to take the train to DC in the morning, and Bud was going to drive her to Penn Station with her luggage to send her off. They'd been staying at a small hotel near the NYPD offices. Without luggage to haul around, she could meet with Jimmy Dimmer unencumbered.

It was time for Rosa to take the subway to the village jazz club. If all went as planned, she'd arrive at five o'clock.

As she climbed the subway stairs to the street, to her surprise, Dr. Dimmer stood waiting at the head of the stairs. He didn't recognize Rosa, and she deliberately bumped into him.

"Oh, I'm so sorry," she told him, taking his arm to steady herself.

He looked at her intently. "I know you!" he said. "You're that detective."

"Yes. I'm that detective, Jimmy. I'm also Maria!" she told him.

"You're kidding, right?" he asked, somewhat confused by this turn of events.

"No, I'm dead serious. My goal was to help you. I wanted you to understand how much trouble you could be in if you refused to believe the authorities," she explained.

"So you disguised yourself, lured me in, and now you want me to meet with you?" His voice was amazed, but he was torn between his Maria and Rosa! Maybe she could help after all. This might work out for him, he thought. "Do you even like jazz?"

"I love jazz, and I hope you will spend some time with me at the jazz club tonight before I leave for DC in the morning."

"You do?" He was taken aback by Rosa's honesty.

"No more lies," she promised him.

He studied this woman who had fooled him so totally and found himself curious and a little amused.

They walked away from the subway entrance and headed toward the jazz club. Jimmy struggled with his mixed emotions. He liked her, but he wasn't sure he could trust her!

Chapter 29

DETECTIVE SYLVIA SANTOS WAS GOING to work the lighthouse murder case through to the end, whatever that was going to be. She was working with the state prosecutor, one of the best in the state, John Rolling. It was time for Sylvia and John to meet again with the defendant and the state-appointed defense attorney. The hearing had not gone well for Jake Dimmer. He was being held without bail. His lawyer was trying to convince him that a plea bargain would be the way to go in this case. He was telling his client that the state's case against him was very strong from the evidence he had seen and that it would be difficult to win against the state. He wanted Jake to realize that life in prison without the possibility of parole was a very long time.

Jake and his attorney, Peter Watch, sat at a table across from Detective Sylvia Santos and John Rolling. Sylvia was offering a deal to avoid a trial.

"Jake, the state is ready to offer you a deal by reducing the charges from murder to manslaughter. This means that you might be able to prove accidental death of your friend. You need to be honest about what actually happened the night you were with Arthur Milne. Do you understand?" Santos asked.

"How many times do I have to tell you that you have the wrong twin? I am innocent," he professed again.

"So you want to go to trial and take your chances that a jury will believe your story?" Prosecutor Rolling asked Jake.

"Yes. I was in Philadelphia, not Provincetown. How could I have done such a thing?" Jake asked, refusing to believe that his person in Philadelphia had told the authorities that he hadn't arrived until midnight Sunday evening of the weekend in question, in essence, voiding his alibi.

"You do know that your story is full of holes?" Detective Santos asked the defendant.

"I'm done here," Jake said to his attorney. "I want to go back to my cell."

"Think about it, Jake. You are giving up a chance to get a good deal. Don't throw it away because you think that you can outsmart the law. You can't," scolded the prosecutor.

The defense attorney looked at Rolling and acknowledged the message.

"I'll work on this with him. What kind of a time window do we have to take the deal?" Peter Watch asked as Jake stood with the guard outside the conference room.

"Short. Time is of the essence," Rolling answered.

"Thanks. We'll be in touch," Watch told the prosecutor.

Jake was of another mind. He was bullheaded and had convinced himself that he would beat the charge. His whole life was a success story of lies. He thought that this was a small blip in his journey. No matter what his lawyer said, Jake was deaf to anything but being exonerated at a trial.

****

Later that day, Jake was summoned to the visitors' area of the prison where he was being held. His twin brother waited to see him.

The two identical twins peered at each other's faces through a glass partition, as though looking into a mirror. Both smiled at the appearance of the other. It seemed to be a long time since all of this life-changing drama had begun.

"They wouldn't let me see you when you were in the infirmary," Jim began.

"They didn't want you to see how they had knocked me around."

"Jake, they said that you did yourself the harm," Jim told him.

"And you believe them and not your brother?" Jake persisted.

"They have a video of you." Jim continued to give Jake the opportunity to tell the truth.

"You and I both know that they can fabricate a video," he said with a tremor.

"Jake, you need to stop lying. Do you hear me?"

"Don't tell me that you believe them with all their lies and false evidence," he hissed.

"I only know that you are in deep trouble. Murder, Jake, you are being accused of murder!"

"Are you a total fool? You don't think for one minute that I am going down for something that *you* did, do you?" Jake smiled a cynical, evil smile at his brother.

"Oh no! Not this time. You will not frame me this time, Jake. You and I know that I am not guilty of this crime. But only you know the truth about yourself—and you need to tell the truth!"

"Go away. I don't need you. I will visit you in jail."

Jim was speechless. It was true what his lawyer had told him. Jake was framing him for a crime he didn't commit. He became angry. His brother needed mental health care. He was out of his mind. He was sick. The authorities were right. Jake was out of touch with reality.

On his way home, Jim phoned his attorney.

"Barry, I've just visited with Jake. He is mounting a case against me. He is accusing me of the murder," he told him with a quivering voice.

"Stay calm. The evidence is strong against your brother. We'll put together an equally strong case to clear your name," the attorney told him.

For a moment Jim felt a surge of confidence.

Jimmy phoned Rosa. Their evening at the jazz club had been more than he had hoped for. They had talked and talked, and he felt that he could trust her. She was very special, and as they talked, he believed that she could help him clear his name.

"Rosa, when can we meet again? I need your professional help, and I'd like to see you again," he said when she answered her phone in the DC office of RAID.

"Jim, I may be able to help you by phone, or you can work directly with FBI Agent Bud Black," she told him.

"But I thought that you wanted to be involved in proving my innocence."

"You have an excellent lawyer, and the case against Jake is very strong as far as I know. I can give my opinion, but I really cannot get involved beyond what I have already done," she said.

"Oh. I guess I misread you, our relationship."

"Listen to me. I wanted justice for you, and I believe that you will be exonerated in all of this. My intentions were purely to get your trust. I am a cop. I was working with the FBI at the time. You are in good hands. If you need my advice, I can do that."

Jimmy felt his spirits fall.

"Thanks, Rosa. I understand and I believe you. Everything will be all right. This nightmare with Jake will soon be over."

It was time for reality. His short-lived fantasy of Rosa was at an end. She was out of his reach.

Chapter 30

STATE PROSECUTOR ROLLING WAS ON the telephone to Defense Attorney Peter Watch regarding the plea bargain offered to his client, Jake Dimmer, in the lighthouse murder case.

"I understand that the state psychiatrist's exam points to a sane person accused of what may have been an accidental death," Attorney Watch was saying.

"We are considering the report's findings, but have not changed the charge of murder," Rolling told him.

"You realize that the report is going to make it almost impossible for you to achieve a first-degree murder charge in court," Watch said.

"What are you offering?" Rolling countered.

"Accidental death, and my client will give his permission to release the doctor's report to you," Watch answered. "We'd like time served against eight years."

"Unrealistic. Manslaughter with twelve years minus time served and a confession. Get back to me on this, and thanks for moving as quickly as you have," Rolling told Watch.

John Rolling hung up the receiver and thought about the conversation with Peter Watch. The psychiatrist's report had become a serious block for the prosecution. If one was to believe anything Jake Dimmer said, he had yet to admit to the crime, with the exception of what the doctor reported. Dimmer had to confess for the plea bargain to work, and that seemed highly unlikely.

John decided to call Detective Sylvia Santos in Provincetown to go over the case he was preparing. Until he saw a confession from Jake Dimmer, he assumed the case would go to trial.

"Hello, John. Nice to hear from you," Sylvia said to him. "Any news?" she asked.

"Hi. I wanted to alert you to a plea bargain offer from the defense attorney that I received today," he told her.

"Did Dimmer confess?" she asked.

"In a matter of speaking he did through his psychiatrist, which is privileged and not available unless Jake Dimmer signs a confession and verifies the reported information," John told her.

"Then we have nothing," Santos commented.

"True, but we do know that with this information, getting a murder charge and conviction looks pretty bleak."

"I'd have to agree with you. Should we go for manslaughter?" Santos asked.

"My experience tells me that we could get either a manslaughter conviction at trial, or with a fair plea bargain, we could get a conviction and avoid a trial," Rolling told her.

"How likely are we to get a signed confession from Jake?" she asked.

"His attorney is working on that now. If he can, we can proceed with a guilty plea of manslaughter and twelve years," he told her.

"I agree. I don't think that this case is premeditated murder. I think the boys were out of control and the unexpected happened and someone died," she confessed to John. "I think that all of this will come out at a trial, and knowing what I know about Jake, this would be too mortifying, too embarrassing. We should push for a plea bargain," Santos told Rolling.

"Thanks. I'll let you know what I hear from Peter on our offer," he said as the conversation ended. He liked to win cases, and he would win this one for the state no matter which way it went. He was leaning toward the plea bargain, knowing how messy this type of case could be and how sensational it could turn.

Chapter 31

BUD NEEDED A BREAK. HE had been working nonstop. A weekend in DC with Rosa had been planned, and he was on his way. Rosa smiled at Bud as he came down the corridor from the train arrivals. He spotted her right away and smiled back.

"How was the train ride?" she asked him.

"Great. I love train rides," he admitted, carrying a small overnight bag over his shoulder.

"Hungry?" Rosa asked. Bud was beginning to show a bit of gray at his temples. She liked that.

"Could eat a horse," he answered, immediately groaning at his poor choice of metaphors.

"I know of a tearoom near here. I've always wanted to try it. Are you game?" Rosa showed her mischievous side as they both groaned at her use of the word *game*.

They were enjoying the wordplay and each other. They would deal with the serious issues later.

The tearoom was charming, the service good, and the food okay. They chatted at the table with small talk. The weather was pleasant, and both were up for a walk after their brunch. They took the long way about the city to get to Rosa's car. When they got to the car, they headed for Independence Mall. Rosa was lucky to find a parking space near the Smithsonian. It was a good location for the start of their walk along the mall.

"Do you like jazz?" Rosa asked him as they walked in the direction of the Capitol building.

Bud was surprised at the question. Rosa knew him for a long time, yet this was the first time she asked something personal. It was refreshing.

"I can enjoy jazz. You know, my life is work right now. I enjoy Broadway shows when I can. This is the first weekend in some time that I have had some downtime," he admitted.

"I hope that you also like classical music. Tonight I have tickets for the Vienna Philharmonic playing a Mozart concert on one of their rare US visits," Rosa told him.

"I can't wait. It will be my first time in years in a concert hall, and my first time hearing the Vienna Philharmonic," he told her.

The day had sped by after walking a good portion of Independence Mall, sitting on benches here and there, and doing their share of people watching along the way back to the car. They had just enough time to grab something to eat, freshen up, and get to the concert.

It was after the concert in a small café that Bud brought up the Dimmer case.

"I'm very concerned. It may look bad for Jimmy Dimmer. You do believe that he's innocent, don't you?" he asked.

Rosa was taken aback by the question. She was convinced that Jimmy was being set up by his twin brother. She wondered why Bud had asked that question. They had agreed that he was innocent, hadn't they?

"Yes, I believe that he is innocent. Why do you ask?" Rosa answered.

"I wonder if you could make an exception with this case. Could I refer Jimmy Dimmer's lawyer to you if need be?" he asked.

"You know that RAID doesn't do this type of work. We are subcontracted by the FBI, CIA, Interpol, and the like to solve international cases with them. You are asking me to work with a personal attorney. I can't do that," she explained.

"Actually, I had a call from Jimmy. He wants me to hire you," Bud told her.

"No, you can't hire me for him," she answered.

"Why not? You were working with me, and I'm FBI," Bud nudged.

"Can we agree to disagree on this? I hate to ruin an otherwise lovely day and evening with an argument," Rosa told him. It was not negotiable.

Bud reluctantly gave up for the time being. He agreed that the day and evening had been too lovely to end on a sour note. He would rethink his approach. For now, he would enjoy the company of this beautiful woman.

Chapter 32

JAKE REQUESTED TO SEE DR. Frick again. He had found the meeting with him helpful. He liked the doctor. Actually, he found him very attractive. He needed to have another session with him. Maybe the doctor could help him find a way out of this whole business.

"Why can't I see Dr. Frick again?" Jake yelled into the telephone to his state-appointed lawyer, Peter Watch.

"He is not a private shrink, Jake. He works for the state of Massachusetts. His job is done with you, until we go to trial," he told him.

"I thought that we were not going to trial," Jake told his attorney.

"That is entirely up to you. The prosecution has offered a plea bargain: your confession for manslaughter and twelve years," Watch told him.

"Oh, I see. I confess, and my brother walks away scot-free. Is that it?" Jake asked.

"Jake, it is not clear to me what your brother did. Can you explain that?" Watch asked.

"He knew everything about Arthur. He met Arthur first. He provided the drugs. He started the whole thing. It is his fault that any of this has happened." Jake fabricated again.

"Was Jimmy present when Arthur died?" Watch asked point-blank.

"No. What difference does that make? He introduced us. He started it," Jake shouted like a child.

"Okay. Can you write down the events that led up to the accident?" Watch asked Jake.

"Yes. I can do that if it will help me out of this mess. Jimmy is not innocent," he reminded Watch.

"Jake, I want to save your life. The plea bargain offered is the best we can get without a trial. I fear that a trial will be very embarrassing for all concerned. The media feeds on stuff like this. I'll come to see you this afternoon. We can work on your statement," he told Jake.

"Okay. Just remember, Jimmy is not clear in all of this," Jake restated.

The phone call ended. Jake was planning his statement to entangle Jimmy.

Defense Attorney Watch was gathering his things for his visit with Jake. He was hopeful that he could get a statement from Jake and put this mess to bed. This was the kind of case that Watch tried to avoid. It had all the makings of sensationalism. If it could be settled quietly, everyone would win, in his opinion.

At two in the afternoon, Attorney Watch was sitting with his client in a room with a table. He offered Jake a pad and pen. Jake took the pad and pen, pulled the chair closer to the table, got comfortable, and began to write. Attorney Watch was unsure what to expect. He sat back in his chair across from Jake and held his breath.

Jake wrote pages and pages of his version of the events that had led up to the accident. He implicated Jimmy whenever he could. He blamed Jimmy for bad drugs the night of the accident that led to his loss of dexterity and inability to loosen the belt around Arthur's neck. He accused Jimmy of causing the accident. After completing his statement and signing it, he handed it to Attorney Watch.

"Here you are. Do what you are supposed to do—defend me!" Jake demanded.

His attorney began to read the statement of ten handwritten pages. He noticed that Jake agreed that he could not loosen the belt around Arthur's neck, causing the death of his lover, but Jake implicated Jimmy as often as he could. He did not want to go down for this accident alone.

Attorney Watch had what he needed for the plea bargain. He had a signed confession from Jake, something no one had expected would ever happen. Whatever had transpired between Jake and Dr. Frick, something had changed Jake's attitude. In his own way, he was taking responsibility for the death of Arthur Milne—finally.

****

State Prosecutor John Rolling thanked Attorney Watch for his effort in securing the confession. The state would proceed with the agreement on manslaughter and a date for a sentencing hearing.

John called Sylvia Santos in Provincetown to tell her where the case was going.

"This is very good news, John," Sylvia said. "I'll let the others know where we are in the case. Thanks."

Sylvia placed a call to Bud Black.

"Hi, Bud. Just thought that you'd like to know that Jake Dimmer wrote and signed a confession today. We are proceeding with a revised charge of manslaughter. The judge will set the term limit at the hearing. Thanks for all the work that you and Rosa did on this case with us. There is one curious thing about the confession. Jake has implicated his twin brother as the reason for the accident in the first place. He said that it was Jimmy who introduced them, provided the drugs, and was just as guilty as he was in causing the accident. He doesn't want Jimmy to walk on this. Any thoughts?" she asked Bud.

"Let me think about this. Rosa has been in touch with Jimmy. Maybe she'll have some thoughts. I'll get back to you. Good to hear your voice. Thanks for the update," Bud said as the call ended.

There seemed to be some loose ends. If Jake was to be believed, what should be done with the information and accusation of Jimmy Dimmer? Santos's ideas were just beginning to form. She looked forward to input from Bud and Rosa on this crease in the case.

****

Two days later, Bud called Sylvia with his update on Rosa's status report on Jimmy.

"Rosa has had several conversations with Jimmy Dimmer regarding the new allegations from his brother. Jimmy denies that there is any truth to his brother's fantasies. He returned to New York after the whale watch trip that Saturday afternoon. He had his canceled bus ticket to prove it. Personally, based on what I know about Jake's propensity to avoid telling the truth, I find Jake's story difficult to believe. Even if it was true, Jimmy is not guilty of murder, accidental or otherwise. I think that it is a stretch to accuse Jimmy. Evidence as far as I know just does not support Jimmy's involvement. With New York's case against Jake for attempted murder of his brother, I think that Jake needs to rethink his story of Jimmy's involvement. Also, he needs to rethink why he says that Jimmy tried to commit suicide, another lie. We think that the lighthouse murder is solved and that the rightfully accused has confessed," Bud told Sylvia. "The FBI has evidence of a connection between Jake and a drug cartel in South America, the source of his unaccounted-for wealth hidden in numerous offshore accounts. It seems more likely that Jake provided the drugs, not Jimmy. Jake is in for a long line of charges, state and federal. I think that Jimmy needs to recover his life, start fresh, and put this behind him. I'm satisfied that we have the truth of what happened, why it happened, and who committed the crime," he added before the conversation ended.

Detective Sylvia Santos hung up the receiver and pushed her chair back away from her desk. What if Jake was telling the truth this time? What if Jimmy started the whole thing by introducing Jake to Arthur? She wondered. On second thought, Jake met Arthur at a tea dance in Provincetown. Yes, they had the right guy. She needed to read up on compulsive liars and sociopaths.